ACCLAIM

"Readers looking for clean YA fantasy will find it in AJ Skelly's *Of Flame & Frost*. I found the story to be a refreshing take on magic school, teens with powers, and opposites attracting. With the right amount of romance and heat, I recommend this book for those wanting a good solid magical story."

—MORGAN L. BUSSE, bestselling and award-winning author of the *Ravenwood Saga* and *Skyworld* series

"With her noteworthy prose filled with wit and charm, Skelly delivers another adventurous yet heart-warming tale. When opposites of fire and ice combine in *Of Flame & Frost*, Skelly teaches readers a valuable lesson that, rather than dividing us, our differences make us stronger."

—V. ROMAS BURTON, bestselling and award-winning author of the *Heartmaker Trilogy*

"AJ Skelly crafts a fast-paced, magic-filled read with dynamic protagonists and a delightful romance that will keep you on your toes and rooting for Aspen and Cole to the final page."

—ALYSSA ROAT, award-winning author of *The Wraithwood Trilogy*

"Spellbinding and filled with adventure, *Of Flame & Frost* hits all the right notes for a fantasy boarding school romance with Skelly's trademark clean but sizzling chemistry, colorful and vivid magic, and fearfully fantastical creatures. I didn't want to leave the enchanting world of Magik Prep even as I turned pages way too fast! You will not want to put this delightful story down!"

—BRITTANY EDEN, bestselling author of *Wishes* and the *Heartbooks* series

Acclaim for The Wolves of Rock Falls series

"...this is a tantalizing read that hooked me from the get go. Skelly flips all the classic shifter tropes upside down and offers a subtly familiar but also uproariously different read from anything I've read in this genre."

—ASTRID V. J., USA TODAY bestselling author of *The Wordmage's Tales* series

"I'm still in awe at the way AJ combines the wolf inside each character."

—BRENDA PANDOS, bestselling author of *The Mer Tales*

"This [*Sworn Shift*] might be my favorite Rock Falls books...I can't decide. All I know is....I love it. It has the perfect level of angst. A touch of steam at doesn't go over the edge. Suspense. Romance. Murder. Misunderstandings. And of course, WOLVES."
—ANNE J. HILL, owner of Twenty Hills Publishing

"Integrity wins over arrogant treachery. Friendship rules, and love is worth waiting and fighting for. Seeing the good guys employ smart, clever tactics was wonderful."
—JASON McCOY, book reviewer

OF FLAME & FROST

OF FLAME & FROST

Quill & Flame
PUBLISHING HOUSE

AJ SKELLY

ALSO BY AJ SKELLY

The Wolves of Rock Falls:

First Shift (2021)
Rogue Shift
Sworn Shift
Dark Shift
Pack Shift
Lost Shift

Making Magik: A Magik Prep Anthology

Murder at Mistlethwaite Manor

Also by April J. Skelly

A Lethal Engagement

Scire Potui
And for the dancing and the dreaming.

"And who knows whether you have not come to the kingdom for such a time as this?"
-Mordecai of Susa

CHAPTER I

ASPEN

Shadows lengthened in the darkening night, dancing and writhing with the bodies on the island.

"Come on, Aspen," Kasin said, tugging my hand. His cool blue eyes twinkled down at me as his perfect lips curved in a winning smile.

My knees went weak as the full force of that smile turned on me.

"I want to show you something." His lips tickled my pointed ear as he whispered. His hand snaked around the small of my back, guiding me down the path, away from the bonfire and the groups of dancing teenagers.

"Aspen, come dance with us!" one of the nymph girls called from a circle of twirling students. Her lithe, nearly translucent form swayed to the music. Curls of magic amplified the noise, setting the beat thumping in my chest. Kasin squeezed my hand as my heart picked up another notch. Parties on the island were common on the weekends. We needed a break from boarding school every now and then. But this was the first one I'd ever been to with Kasin.

"Maybe later," I called with a wave of my hand. The nymph winked at me, fluttering her long fingers.

"Kasin! They're setting up a game of catch the pixie! We had a freshman pixie volunteer! We can't let that go," an elf with ears pierced five times called.

"You can catch him on your own," Kasin called back with a grin.

"What? You're missing out!"

"Not this time," Kasin said softly to me as he tugged me deeper into the shadows surrounding several of the old buildings that dotted the island in the middle of the Chasm.

This was my first date with Kasin. We were both at the height of popularity at Magik Prep Academy and made quite the couple. Tongues had started wagging and gossip trembled down the magic strings the second we stepped foot on the Island together for tonight's party. I secretly hoped he had a romantic picnic set up in one of the buildings—a midnight snack just for the two of us. Frost tingled at the ends of my fingertips at the thought.

Kasin tugged an age-worn door open, lightly pushing me inside.

"What did you want to show me?" I asked as the door shut behind him, plunging us into darkness.

I could feel the heat coming off him as he stepped into my space. "This," he whispered as his lips covered mine.

Oh.

Part of me was disappointed that Kasin just wanted to make out. Not that I didn't enjoy being kissed, but I had hoped for a little more romance. For several minutes, his lips moved against mine, his arms holding me close.

Then, almost like a switch had flipped, his hands gripped me harder, sending my pulse spiking. Pushing against me with his hips, he backed me up until my back hit the rough wooden wall. His lips were hard, insistent. His hands found my hips, squeezing, dipping lower. I was not enjoying this anymore.

"Kasin," I dragged my lips away from the onslaught of his, trying to push him away. "Stop. I'm done."

"No, you're not. You've been flirting with me for weeks. All night you've been staring at me with those eyes. You've been telling me you wanted this since the second we stepped foot on the Chasm bridge," he growled the words, pushing harder against me, his hands slipping up the sides of my shirt.

Ice crackled in my chest as fury radiated cold to my fingertips.

"I said *no*."

I grabbed his wrist, but he shook me off, the bulk of his body pinning me to the wall. Anger and fear twisted maliciously in my gut. Squirming, I pushed against him. I might as well have been a sprite trying to take down an ogre.

"I know you want this. You're going to give me what you've been teasing." Lust practically leaked out of his pores as my heart galloped into my throat. This was bad. *Really bad.*

Black pin pricks dotted the outside of my vision as he rammed his shoulder into my solar plexus, keeping me from escaping as he undid the fly of his jeans.

Frost crept over my pillow, over the edge of my comforter. My heart pounded. My legs tried to run—run away—but I was stuck fast. He loomed over me. Terror and anger clouded my vision and the frost flowing from my fingers became ice. His hand swept towards me with fingers outstretched like claws.

I woke panting, heart drumming. A fine layer of ice crystals covered my blanket under my fingertips. A dream. It was only a dream. A dream wreathed in memory. Memory of what was—and what could have been.

Kasin was a boil on the backside of a pookah.

Blinking blearily, I rubbed the corners of my eyes. Squinting at the dial on my bedside table, I resisted the urge to groan, and forced my legs over the edge of my bed. The cold stone floor didn't bother me in the least, but I missed the warmth of my covers. Just because I was a frost fairy didn't mean I didn't like the heat. Shaking my head, I tried to leave the last vestiges of the memory-dream behind.

Trudging down the dormitory corridor to the communal bathroom, I paused as voices echoed into the ancient stone hallway. Knowing I probably shouldn't, I snagged a little piece of bright-colored magic that hovered near me, bending it to amplify what the girls were saying. Right as I finished contorting it, a shower turned on and I rolled my eyes. Flicking the magic away, I shuffled into the bathroom.

Tall and gorgeous, Tawny Evrel, and her side kick, short squatty Arietta Gowan, looked at me in the reflection of the mirror. The two biggest gossips at Magik Preparatory Academy. Arietta tittered and my stomach dropped to my toes.

"Honey, if you were that nervous, you could have asked me for some tips. I would have gladly shared." Tawny winked at me, though the gesture lacked kindness.

My white-blonde eyebrow rose. "Um, thanks," I said before ignoring them, swallowing hard, and heading to an empty shower stall. Arietta giggled behind her hand and that niggling finger of concern wiggled in my middle.

The refectory hushed as I came through the doors. The weight of the stares suddenly directed at me sat on my shoulders like a giant's hand pressing me into the earth. My fingers twitched as frost began forming on the underside of my tray without my permission. Why was everyone staring at me? My heart picked up, my pulse growing painfully pronounced.

Whispers began circulating like dragonfire, spreading from one table to the next.

Ice Queen, the whispers said.

Frost morphed into little chips of ice. My tray groaned. The whispers weren't referring to my ability to create ice on demand. My stomach plunged to my toes as I forced my chin into the air.

I turned to my regular table where my circle of friends sat, a collection of fae and a few other species. Before I could sit, Laara gave me a look of pity that made my toes curl.

"What?" I snapped irritably. I had no idea what everyone thought they knew about me. But as dread crept up my spine, I was willing to bet a season's snowfall that it had to do with Kasin Geethon. That smarmy toad.

"It's okay. We all know," Laara said, her eyes holding pity and a hint of embarrassment that bordered on predatory.

"Know what?" I ground out. My fingers bit into the shards of ice coating the underside of my tray.

"What happened at the party Saturday night," she whispered. Her eyes held the sort of wild delight that let me know whatever the grapevine said was salacious, juicy, and scandalous. And undoubtedly not the truth. My eyes narrowed as frost crept up the sides of my tray.

"What did Kasin say?" I asked through clenched teeth.

"Everyone is nervous their first time." Laara's saccharine voice grated my skin like sandpaper.

Anger boiled inside me, and I knew I needed to get outside where I could safely vent the ice that was going to blast out my fingers if I didn't release some tension *soon*.

I dropped my tray of untouched food onto the table. It cracked in half on impact. Turning on my heel, I stormed back out the doors. Snickers and a cat call followed me until the heavy oak door swooshed shut behind me.

Once I was in the courtyard, blessedly devoid of other students, I dug my fingers into the soft grass and let my frustration flow out of my fingers. Little raised bumps fractured away from my hands as ice displaced the dirt, leaving a long shaft of frozen frustration burrowing into the ground.

I straightened from my crouch and watched as Arietta crossed the far side of the lawn. My fingers curled into tight fists as her short legs clipped across the grass towards another girl exiting the refectory. Arietta's eyes were fairly sparking with a sort of fevered glow as she not so surreptitiously jerked her head towards me.

With a single flick of my wrist, I brought a cold wind whistling down from the eves and brought her hushed words to my ears.

"Yes, that's her. Aspen Frost. Kasin said she was so nervous after he kissed her that she literally froze her own thighs shut. Can you imagine? How humiliating! And after she's been leading Kasin on for weeks!"

Rage consumed me as a shower of snowflakes blanketed the roof.

CHAPTER 2

COLE

The girls stared as I trudged down the stone hallway beneath the gothic-styled arches where strings of magic floated. All fire-drakes were alluring in their human form, though my mother's phoenix blood made me taller and slenderer than most. I gulped and made sure my mask of indifference was firmly in place. My hands clenched into fists inside the pockets of my magic-lined pants. I willed the flames that licked under my skin to settle. Anxiety still rippled up my spine. Blinking, I hoped my inner fire wasn't showing in my eyes.

The office was at the center of the building and it took half an age to get there. All the while, the stares of students burned into my back like hot irons. I hated being the new kid. But Magik Prep was my last chance. I'd been to three other lesser schools closer to home. To no avail. Magik Prep was supposed to be the best. If I couldn't learn how to control my fire here, then I'd be dangerous and alone the rest of my life. And that thought set my teeth on edge and my heart plummeting to my toes.

Maybe a monster like me deserved to live in isolation.

It didn't matter. At least, that's what I told myself as I put another brick in the wall around my heart. My walls were my defense. With an arrogant tilt of my chin, I tossed my black hair out of my eyes and opened the door to the office, careful not to touch the brass handle long enough it overheated.

"Good morning," a cheerfully plump woman greeted me. Tiny little horns poked through her curly hair. Her face was a veneer of heavy-handed makeup, but her eyes were genuine enough. She got up from behind her desk and tromped over to me on little goat feet.

"Here, dear, come right through here. You must be Cole? Cole Raiden?" She extended her arm to usher me in but was careful to keep her distance. At least there was no fear in her eyes. Yet.

I nodded and walked where she indicated.

"We'll just get you settled. I'm Ms. Pennywiggle."

I stifled a snort. Pennywiggle? She ignored my ill manners and rifled through a folder on a desk.

"There now. I've got your schedule here and a map of the school."

She handed the papers out to me. I stared at them.

"Don't you want to take them?"

My face flushed and fire raged through me, hot and uncontrolled.

"I can't," I grunted.

"Oh." Her eyes widened. "*Oh*." She tapped her lip with a red manicured nail. "What did you do at your last school?"

I swallowed down as much shame as I could. "If you could lay them out on the desk, I'll look at them there."

She looked at me uncertainly but did as I asked. I smothered a sigh. I'd taught myself to memorize quickly years ago. I had to do something since flammable things turned to ash in my hands.

I studied my schedule then the layout of the school. Once I knew I had it down I nodded to Ms. Pennywiggle.

Orange light zinged down the office ceiling making me flinch.

"Don't worry about that, dear. It's just the magic. It's been laying around for centuries. We use it as we need it. The orange flash means ten increments until class starts. Do you want me to get an office aide to help you to your first class?"

No. No, I really did not want an office aide showing me to first period.

"I'll be fine," I said brusquely.

I shouldered my backpack, also woven with magic so it wouldn't catch fire every time I touched it, and slouched through the doors.

Careful to avoid contact with anyone, I moved down the hallway with serpentine grace and an arrogant smirk on my face that never failed to attract the girls and annoy the guys. I hoped my black clothes and equally dark expression would act as deterrent enough for people to leave me alone.

I was a powder keg waiting for the tiniest spark. That's all it would take for me to raze this place to the ground.

CHAPTER 3

ASPEN

I couldn't handle the refectory again. All morning whispers of *Ice Queen* and stifled giggles had raced around me. Kasin wasn't even at school today. I knew why. But my side of the story was too little too late. Kasin got there first and made sure nobody would believe the truth if I told them. Rage threatened to turn into tears. Stopping in an empty alcove off the hallway, I closed my eyes, and willed the tears away. I would not give him the satisfaction of a single tear, rage-induced or not. I took a deep inhale. Dust, age-worn stone, and the fizzy tingle of magic calmed me. These were the smells I'd grown up with.

My belly growled, reminding me that I'd skipped breakfast. I bit my lip and left the alcove. Digging in my bag I found a few coins and felt the tension ebb as I counted out enough for some hydra jerky and an everflower juice from the hallway vending machines.

Taking my meager lunch with me, I pushed through the doors and into the fresh cool air of the clois-ters. The cloisters were a beautiful open-arched encircled square of lawn, magicked green year-round. Even when the snows fell, it was kept clear and stayed fresh. The ancient stone columns surrounding the grass vaulted into their finely wrought points where carved stone creatures of myth and legend danced in and out, keeping eternal watch on the middle of the lawn. Sloping down to the side of the cloisters was the green. A stretch of meadow-like land tucked away in the corner of the towering stone walls that surrounded the entire school. Farther beyond the walls was the Chasm.

My belly clenched and a shiver worked over my shoulders as I looked out at the island surrounded by jagged cliffs of rock that time and the river had eroded. If only I hadn't let him talk me into going to that party on the island Saturday night. I shook my head, shoved the memories back down, and marched towards the green.

Sitting on the grass, I ignored the chill wind that swept over the walls, adjusting my body temperature to match the icy blast, and cracked open my ever-flower juice. My eyes closed as the sweet tangy liquid settled over my tongue. The refrigerated can was warmer than the cold air outside, so the juice felt warm as it slid down my throat.

Glancing around, I startled faintly. The new guy—whispers about the aloof handsome newcomer had reached even my pariah's ears—sat just on the other side of the cloisters on the green. We weren't terribly far apart, but far enough that we weren't within speaking distance.

Suddenly he turned his head and his eyes pierced me. They were black. Cold, hard, onyx surrounded by milky white. His face was pale under the sweep of coal-colored hair and his lanky arms were propped up on his knees. He had a killer jaw line, sharp and angled. His nose was straight and perfect. I blinked and dropped my gaze. He was beautiful in a terrifyingly frigid sort of way. I breathed a sigh through my nose and took a bite of my hydra jerky. I briefly wondered if he'd heard rumors about me yet. Loneliness welled up inside me as the meat in my mouth turned into gelatinous sludge. I blinked back sudden forlorn tears, unwilling to let myself come undone out here. I'd wait until tonight when I could scream my silent rage into my pillow back at the dormitory.

I missed my best friend. Mykeltie had left last week to go on her annual family foraging trip. As earth fae, they needed to spend time in nature away from people and other creatures. I wished her family trip hadn't fallen right now. I'd never needed my best friend more. It felt like the whole world had turned against me. Mykeltie never would though. At least she wouldn't be bothered by my misery in our shared dormitory room or be tainted by her association to me.

Sighing, I angrily snatched a few blades of grass. My gaze swung again to the island jutting up from the

Chasm. I wanted to send lightning bolts from my eyes and blast it to smithereens. If only I could. Instead, I put my palms on the ground and sent rivulets of ice into the earth that raised tiny molehills around me. Orange light flickered in the windows to my left, and I knew my respite was over.

I drank the rest of my juice and swallowed down the rest of the jerky. Brushing my palms together to rid any lingering frost, I gathered my bag and glanced again at the new boy. He still sat, looking straight ahead. He had to know I was there, but he made no move to acknowledge my presence. Everything about him screamed *dangerous*.

With a miniscule shake of my head, I took a breath and forced myself to put one foot in front of the other towards my next class.

CHAPTER 4

COLE

So far, I'd managed to avoid all contact and made only terse comments in class when forced to. I waited until the last minute at lunch, taking in the stillness of the open spaces and the cold air that had been a relief from the stifling heat of indoors, before heaving to my feet and heading back inside. Lunch outside would have been pleasant except for the girl who came and sat outside, too. I was concerned that she'd try to talk to me. There was always a girl at every school that tried to be my savior, bring me out of my shell, tame the bad boy. Fortunately, this girl had been happy to leave me alone.

The door to history was open so I didn't have to fear super heating the handle for the next student. Although I needn't have worried. I was the very last one. The door shut behind me automatically as a zing of green magic stuttered through the hall.

Professor Rashtin, I remembered from my schedule, stood at the front of the room. His horse body was perfectly groomed while the upper human part of him was clothed in a neat suit jacket and tie. Without a word but with a kind look, he pushed up his spectacles then motioned for me to take the only seat left in the room. Towards the back and right next to the girl from the green.

She looked up at me. Her clear blue eyes showed her surprise as her pale eyebrows lifted. Quickly she dropped her gaze back to her notebook. Careful not to touch anyone as I inched down the aisle between the rows, I sank into my chair, vigilantly keeping my hands from touching the wood. So long as my clothes acted like a barrier, I was safe to sit on regular furniture.

My heart squeezed painfully as I glanced again at the girl next to me. I'd noticed her paleness on the green but forced myself to pay no attention to her. Now that she was right next to me—close enough to touch if I leaned—I shuddered. Something about her reminded me of Syrai. Bricking up the hole that thought punched through my carefully constructed emotional walls, I sat still and gulped as fire rushed through my veins.

Reasoning with myself, I argued that the girl next to me was nothing like Syrai. They didn't even look similar. Syrai had been dark and warm where this girl was all white and ethereal. Silky white-blonde hair fell to the middle of her back. Her fingers were long and slender where they gripped her pen. Syrai...*Syrai*. Just thinking her name brought enough shame and guilt that my fingers clenched in my lap. Regret threatened to swallow me whole.

"If I might draw your notice to this section of the map here." Professor Rashtin addressed the class. I willfully brought my attention back to the present and away from dark memories.

Trudging through the doorway, I sighed. Feeling like I'd been on display all day, I was done being looked at, whispered about, and checked out as I walked down Magik Prep's ancient stone corridors. Classes were done for the day; I'd survived, and even found some of them interesting. I was thankful I'd shared only history with the girl that reminded me of Syrai.

Glancing up, I wanted to groan. I wasn't done being on display yet. A short red-headed girl pumped her legs down the hallway, her gaze fixed on me, a determined dimple set into one cheek.

Ah, here she was. The girl who would try to save me from myself. It was so stupid. You couldn't save a broken monster, and I resented their efforts. I didn't have to work up much energy, because the glare came naturally to my face as soon as the girl opened her mouth. I just wanted to go back to my dorm room, away from the world, and crash. But now I was in the emptying hallway with savior-girl.

"I'm Arietta," the red-headed girl said, her voice full of self-importance. She barely came up to my chest, so she had to tip her head back to see my face. "I wanted to introduce myself and see if there was anything you needed, since you're new and all." She prattled and the beginnings of a headache ghosted up the back of my skull.

"I know everything about everyone, so if there's anything you ever want to know, I'm your girl." She waved her hand in the air dramatically and pointed to herself. "So, you're Cole Raiden. Where are you from?"

Her hand came down like she meant to rest it on my arm. In horror I jerked back.

"Don't touch me," I hissed between my teeth as adrenaline spiked my heartbeat into triple-time. Before I could stop it flames lit my eyes, wreathing my face in a fiery glow that sent ripples of heat radiating from every pore in my body. It was phoenix fire but magnified a hundred-fold because of my mutated genes. It was also mortifying to be nearly eighteen years old and have so little control over myself. Particularly in front of this girl who set my teeth on edge.

"Whoa!" Areitta jumped back. "So, you're *literally* and figuratively hot. Too hot to handle. This school is going to *love* you." Her brown eyes grew stony as a calculating grin covered her mouth. With a flip of her hair, she turned and sashayed back down the hallway leaving me feeling cold despite my frustration and the uncontrollable inferno simmering under my skin.

CHAPTER 5

ASPEN

I was utterly worn by the time I made it back to my dorm room. I snagged a few pieces of light blue magic on my way back and stuffed them into my pockets. Once my door clicked shut, I flipped the lock, took out the magic, and flung it to the four corners of my room. I needed privacy. And magic was the only want to ensure that at this school.

My bag thudded to the floor like it was full of rocks. My shoes landed in a heap outside the closet door. I stood still for a moment, then with abandon, I let myself flop backwards onto my bed. A few ice crystals leaked out as I pressed the heels of my hands to my eyes.

My heart was bruised. I'd liked Kasin. I'd trusted him in the way a girl trusts a part of herself to her crush. And then he'd tried to break me. But I was made of stronger stuff than that. I would not break. Not over this. I sniffed and wiped my eyes.

No one cared about my side of the story. Kasin's version was so sensational, nothing I could say would trump his version. Besides, he was the golden boy. Nothing dark could touch him, though I now knew the ugly truth about Kasin Geethon.

Until this morning, I had been the counterpart golden girl. How quickly one rumor had yanked me from my pedestal. It *hurt*. Like the heavy barbs of a kraken harpoon punched through my chest. I hadn't been expecting the rumor in the first place—and I hadn't expected my so-called friends to turn on me so quickly. Or to believe such a pack of lies. Honestly. I froze my own thighs shut?

I burned with icy frustration, both at his insinuation, and at the part of me that felt guilty and dirty. I had nothing to feel guilty over. Regardless of what the rumors implied. *You have nothing to feel guilty over!* I screamed at myself inside my head. A few more tiny ice chips slid down my cheeks. Angrily, I swiped them away and sat up. With a calming breath, I trudged to the chair in front of the vanity.

It was technically breaking protocol to contact Mykeltie, but I didn't want to call my parents. They'd only worry. But I needed to talk to someone.

I decided I would leave a message for her. That way, if she was in the middle of foraging, or finding a coveted tangle patch mushroom, I wouldn't bother her until she had a chance to respond.

Not five minutes after sending my message on a twangy piece of neon magic, the same laser lemon color blasted across the mirror over our shared vanity and the familiar face of my best friend filled the surface. Her wild dark hair was flung around her head and her too-large ears like a poof of russet dandelion fluff. There was a smudge of darker dirt on her brown cheek and a shine to her luminous dark eyes that told me she'd found her favorite wild berries out in the thicket at some point during the day.

"Aspen!" Her normally soft, low-pitched voice was high and shrill in comparison. "What happened? Are you all right?"

"Hey Keltie." I sighed and sank into the chair, leaving my elbows propped on the vanity. "I've been better. I'm sorry to call you in the middle of your trip, but I needed my best friend."

She snorted. "Of course, you should have called me. Don't be silly. Now tell me everything."

So, I did. My face was flushed and streaked with a few errant ice crystals by the time the whole sordid story was out. I was thankful for the blue tendrils of magic that kept my words inside my room.

"I really thought Kasin was different," Mykeltie said. Her eyes still sparked in anger.

"I did, too."

"Are you horribly upset? I mean, obviously Kasin is an amoebic fungus, but you know, you liked him."

"I did. I don't think I'm as upset about that as I am about the rumors. I don't even care so much what everyone thinks happened—but I can't get away from the pity and the giggles and the...*savagery* of some

people. Can I tell you how much I hate being the vir-
gin slut?" I dropped my face in my hands, momentarily
massaging my aching temples.

"Well, you are in the upper echelons of the school
hierarchy. So is Kasin. It's a long fall to the bottom, which is where he's trying to put you." Mykeltie
always told the truth. She didn't mean it unkindly.
She didn't have an intentionally malicious bone in her
body.

"Well, the mighty have fallen from grace, I assure
you." I tried to keep the bitterness from my tone,
propping my chin on my hand and staring back at my
friend.

"I know you never cared that you were popular. But
other girls like Tawny and Arietta did—do. They want
your spot at the top. They see this as their chance and
they're taking it."

"What do I do now?" My eyes had dried. I'd given
myself my pity party. I needed to haul myself up and
move forward now. My heart was tired but lighter.

"You're going to hold your head up. You've done
nothing wrong. Kasin is the pile of Titanoboa turds.
It's probably going to suck in the meantime, but in
a few weeks, someone else will find their way into
Arietta's clutches and this incident will be forgotten."
She put her hand sympathetically against her side of
the mirror. "Tomorrow when we go out, I'm going to
find some wyrmwood roots. That will fix Kasin nicely.
He'll be stuck in the bathroom for days. Things hap-

pening at both ends." Mykeltie's eyes slitted merrily as a feral grin tipped her lips. Maybe I was wrong. Perhaps she did have a few malicious bones.

A half smile found its way to my face. "We'll talk revenge when you get back," I offered half-heartedly.

"I'm sorry, Aspen." Her regular low-pitched throatiness was back, and it soothed some of my frazzled nerves.

"I know. Thank you for listening. Don't get into trouble hunting up questionable herbs on my behalf."

She giggled. "If I told Luke, he'd help me."

I groaned. "I'm not sure that's a good idea. Your brother likes to take things a bit too far. Hopefully by the time you get back, this will have all blown over."

"I hope you're right. Go get something to eat. I can hear your belly rumbling through the connection."

"Yeah. I think I'm going to order in from The Sun God's Grill. I could really go for a kraken burger and fries. Mm. Extra elixir dipping sauce." It was one of our favorite restaurants from the village near the school. And they delivered directly to the dormitories.

Mykeltie raised an eyebrow. "Head high," she admonished.

"Right. Miss you, Keltie."

"Miss you, too, Aspen. Keep me posted. And connect whenever you need. All right?"

I smiled and held my palm to hers, ending the call. Yellow magic flashed quickly, and I was left staring at my own morose reflection.

I placed an order with The Sun God's Grill.

CHAPTER 6

COLE

Tuesday dragged by. I survived, but I was pretty sure that girl—Arietta—was concocting something with my name involved. I caught her watching me a few times in the hallway and once as I was getting my specialty metal tray of food in the refectory. I still ate outside. I needed the break from prying eyes and the fear of setting things on fire. At least outside, the worst that could happen was that I'd scorch some grass. I could fix that easily with all the magic floating around this place. It was incredible, the magic that randomly breezed by and collected like dust. My other schools had taught me how to use it, but they hadn't had it in abundance like this place. I'd never seen so much, or so many variations of magic, in one place. I chewed a bite of something brown off the tray.

The pale girl sat opposite me again. I wondered why she didn't sit inside with everyone else. She was pretty. More than pretty. I couldn't imagine she had trouble making friends. Carefully, I averted my gaze. I didn't need her to catch me watching her. Nothing like adding *creep* to whatever other words were already attached to me.

Wednesday there was a subtle shift in the atmosphere of the school. As I left my dormitory and made the short walk towards the school building, I saw a small crowd gathered around a caramel-colored head. I slowed and let them enter the building first. They were going toward the lockers, and even though I didn't need to stop at mine, with my curiosity roused, I trailed them. Lounging like I belonged near one of the metal lockers, I watched from the fringes.

Fae, elves, a dryad, and even a young centaur crowded around the boy with the caramel-colored hair. Was he Magik Prep royalty? He said something and the group of them laughed. He pointed across the hall at the opposite bank of lockers, and I was surprised to find the girl from the green.

Glancing back, the group had shifted so that I had a clear view of caramel-hair guy as he mouthed *Ice Queen* towards the girl. Then he made an obscene gesture that set my blood boiling through me, igniting flames and sending sparks racing along my skin. I shifted, making sure my shirt sleeves were pulled all the way down. Regardless of what the girl may have done, this guy was a tool.

Thoughts of Syrai flashed through my head with force enough to make me wince. I wondered if the girl needed help. For a moment I struggled. I shouldn't get involved. I would only make things worse. Monsters made more problems. But something about the girl tugged at me.

Her lips thinned and her eyes narrowed. With a quick flick of her wrist, huge balls of hail pounded down on the tool and his groupies.

Nope. She did not need my help. My eyebrows lifted. I was pretty sure using natural magic—magic produced within certain creatures—was forbidden inside the walls of Magik Prep. My inner fire banked to its normal roar. Her icy gaze met mine across the hall.

I tipped my chin to her, turned, and took myself to class. I couldn't afford to get involved. Not with anyone. That's how people got hurt. And clearly, this girl didn't need my brand of trouble. She had enough of her own.

After school, I had my first session with my mentor. Part of the package deal with my attendance at Magik Prep. I was far from comfortable with the situation. My mentor was supposed to function as one part counselor, one part instructor, and one part trainer. I wasn't sure how well that was going to work since he wasn't a fire-drake. Fire-drakes were incredibly rare anymore. Where they had once populated the tri kingdoms, they'd never reproduced quickly or with great frequency, and their numbers had slowly dwindled. That was part of the reason my father, a fire-drake, had married my mother, a phoenix. Shape shifters took many forms, but not all of them were completely compatible with each other. In my parents' case, flame attracted flame. And I was born with flames I could no longer control.

Mr. Redmond waited in a room that was little more than a rounded stone closet with a window set high in the outside wall to let in some natural light. He had a desk lamp on, and he smiled as I opened the door.

"Cole. It's good to meet you again. How have your first few days gone?" He came from behind his desk to perch on the edge of it. His full beard was dark and well kempt, and his khakis were pressed with a crease down the center fold. I couldn't tell if I was going to like him or hate him.

"Fine." I gave a standard one syllable answer.

Mr. Redmond nodded and stroked a hand over his beard.

"You know, the more you put into these sessions, the more you'll get out of them. But I understand that I'm still a stranger. Why don't you have a seat, and we'll work on getting to know each other better and see if we can come up with some goals we'd like to work on in our next sessions."

I glanced at the chair he indicated. It wasn't metal. And there weren't nearly enough strands of magic wavering over its surface to keep it from bursting into flames should anything other than my clothes touch it.

With a sigh, I dropped my bag near the door and slid down the stone wall onto the cool flagstones of the floor.

"Uh, Cole, why don't you try the chair?"

I looked up at him from my place on the floor. This man didn't understand yet. My clothes would act as a barrier between me and the chair, but that wasn't the point. "Haven't you read my file?"

"Of course, I have. I've made sure the chair is magicked. It should be perfectly fine."

"That chair isn't magicked nearly hard enough."

Mr. Redmond frowned. "Here, watch."

He turned towards the chair and let loose a stream of phoenix fire from his eyes that hit the chair squarely on the seat. Nothing happened. The magic absorbed the white-hot fire and the chair remained intact.

"See? Nothing to worry about." Mr. Redmond smiled good naturedly.

Heaving to my feet I looked him in the eye and put one hand down on the seat. For three seconds nothing happened. Then smoke curled up from around my palm. I jerked my hand back before the whole thing could crumble to ashes.

My palm print, ringed in orange coals and blackened material, stared back up at us as strands of magic shriveled away from the impact of so much direct heat.

"Ah." Mr. Redmond cleared his throat. "Why don't you tell me what you need then?"

Once Mr. Redmond understood my condition better, I grudgingly started to like him more. I reluctantly gave him what details I could. I hated talking about myself and my insecurities. The things I couldn't do.

"So it's been four years since you've had control?"

I nodded miserably. Four years of being a monster out of control.

He stroked his beard again. He'd moved to lean against one of the stone walls, his feet crossed at the ankles, as I slumped in the burned chair, my clothes enough protection against the material now that I'd made my point.

"Cole, I've never mentored anyone in your exact position, granted. But I have worked with a few other people who were cross species."

I bristled at the term, but Mr. Redmond either ignored my reaction or didn't notice it because he continued.

"I think most of your inability to control your fire stems from fear. And also from a lack of self-acceptance. The fear part we'll get to in a later session. But the other part, simply put, you need to accept yourself. You are part fire-drake and part phoenix. You won't be able to control your flames until you accept who you are. Half of two parts that have to come together to make one whole you. There's nothing wrong with being something in the middle of your parents' species."

There was everything wrong with it. *What* I was had determined *who* I became. And I hated who I was. Hated that I hurt everyone around me.

Hated that I had so little hope.

CHAPTER 7

ASPEN

Thursday was exhausting. After I lost my cool on Wednesday and sent a hailstorm down on Kasin in the hallway, which had been momentarily gratifying, I walked on eggshells the rest of the day. If a teacher had seen me, I'd be expelled for a few days, and I had no desire to plummet my grades via expulsion or to make my parents worry. Or incur their disappointment. I still hadn't told them about what had happened with Kasin. I knew I should, but I just didn't have the emotional energy it would take to rehash everything. I'd taken measures into my own hands instead...hence the illegal ice indoors. Anger was easier than hurt, disappointment, and worry.

Kasin hadn't appreciated the hailstorm either. He'd made sure to spread a few more details about my "first time jitters" in the most unflattering way possible. As I was changing books out at my locker, keeping my head down between second and third period, whispers found my pointed ears and stopped my fingers mid-way from putting a book into my bag.

I didn't know who was speaking, but I heard Arietta's trademark scandal beneath the whispers.

"He burned his entire house down. Burned his parents to a crisp in their beds. That's why he's here. He has nowhere else. His court-appointed guardians refused to keep him in the house. Sent him to Magik Prep instead. The Academy is the only place that would take him."

"That's horrendous! I mean, he's gorgeous. It's always the best packages that hide the darkest secrets."

"Right? *Fire Freak*!"

The two girls passed by as an unnatural chill swept through my veins. They had to be talking about the new guy. I wondered how much of Arietta's story was true. I shook my head, clearing thoughts of the still-too-recent rumors running rampant about me. I knew how much of *those* were true. I wondered if Fire Freak stories would replace Ice Queen ones anytime soon. Then I cringed and blushed as shame replaced the iciness that had fallen over me. That was selfish and unkind. I didn't want someone else to suffer the same way I was. But I didn't deny that I wanted my own frustrated misery to end.

Shutting my door and shoving my book into my bag, I legged it down the hallway as neon green magic zinged overhead. I wanted to be in the classroom and out of the line of fire of any more rumors being passed around in the hallways.

History was one of my favorite classes, but my skin prickled as I sank into my seat and saw the boy from lunch—I still didn't know his name—already seated and staring straight ahead. A muscle in his chiseled jaw jumped as he clenched his teeth.

Training my eyes to my notebook, I let my fingers doodle. I could feel the heat radiating off him. *Could* he have incinerated his whole family? That would certainly make me want to shut myself away from the rest of the world. Accidents did happen. I shivered. Pre-meditated murder happened, too.

Professor Rashtin brought the class to order and pointed at one of the many maps dotting the front wall of the classroom.

"We're picking up today with more history of the Academy. As you know, its founding was fraught with much opposition from several sectors of the tri king-doms. King Trindon III, king during the founding of Magik Preparatory Academy, was able to solidify an alliance with his neighbors, and with the help of sever-al founders—some of whom have direct descendants that still go to this school," Professor Rashtin smiled at me.

My face flushed before I could regulate my temper-ature. I didn't need any additional attention drawn to me right now.

"They were able to form Magik Prep. It was a hard-fought formation. Those who didn't agree with the fundamental ideals of Magik Prep—freedom and knowledge for all magical creatures regardless of social caste or race—created opposition for years. There was a battle twenty-five years after the Academy began. A battle that might have been lost had it not been for a fire-drake such that the world has never seen since. Alger-Aodh. He is considered the father of all fire-drakes because of his great age and the wisdom he passed down to all of his kind, not to mention his integral part in winning the war that changed the tide for freedom for all magical species. It is said Alger-Aodh was the biggest fire-drake the known world had ever seen. That this drake alone held off the forces of the enemy so that King Trindon had time to bring in troops to defeat the opposing faction. Legend says Alger-Aodh is the one that melted the glacier that formed the river that runs through the Chasm today."

"Maybe the Fire Freak could melt the Ice Queen!" The whisper might as well have been shouted into the classroom.

My blood turned to ice even as I saw red. I gripped the edges of my desk but couldn't stop the layer of frost that immediately covered the underside.

Professor Rashtin was laying into someone towards the front of the room, his horse tail swishing angrily. But I couldn't hear past the pounding anger in my ears. Frost crept over the sides and onto the top of the desk. I was immobile, powerless to stop the anger that

burned through my fingertips and froze the wooden
slab under them.

CHAPTER 8

COLE

Fire Freak? That was the best they could come up with? It hardly penetrated more than an inch or two beyond the emotional brick walls I set up around myself. But it didn't stop the resentment from bubbling up inside me like lava. Resentment towards the creator of the name, and resentment at myself, which was closely followed by guilt because it inevitably brought thoughts of Syrai to mind.

I swallowed. My hands clenched hard enough my knuckles stood out white against my reddening skin. I snuck a look at the girl beside me. Clearly the whispered words had more effect on her than they did on me.

Her eyes blazed with a palpable chill. My own eyes widened as I heard a soft *creak*. Her hands were clamped against the sides of her desk. A sheen of lacy ice scrolled up over the top, underneath her textbook and her notes. The wood groaned.

She was going to break that desk in half if she didn't stop. I glanced back up at her face. It might as well have been carved from granite.

I don't know if it was the way she subtly reminded me of Syrai or the way I'd seen the group of guys making fun of her this morning, but in an uncharacteristic display of charity, I forced my hand to unclench and eased it carefully through the aisle to the underside of her desk.

The wood was cold and brought an instant sense of relief to my sweltering skin. I placed two fingers gently at the edge of her desk and watched as her frost melted away, leaving a few drips to splash silently onto the floor.

She must have felt the heat through the wood. Her eyes wrenched to mine, wide, blue, and startled. Glancing back down, she seemed to see her desktop for the first time and yanked her fingers off the top of the wood.

Immediately I removed my fingers, clenched them back into a fist, and stared straight ahead, heart pounding.

I didn't dare look at her again during class. The rest of Professor Rashtin's lecture fell on deaf ears as far as I was concerned, even though I truly wanted to hear more about Alger-Aodh.

A weight had dropped onto my shoulders. Ironic. Helping people was supposed to bring satisfaction. Instead, dread settled in my middle as flames thrashed up and down my limbs. Some sort of repercussion was inevitable—whether from the girl herself or from the student who'd unwisely opened their mouth during class. The unknown knotted up my insides. Staying away was how I kept control. If people started approaching me, they'd see the monster underneath. That's when they'd get hurt.

Purple magic lit the hallway, signaling the end of class. Moving as quickly as I was able without touching anyone or anything, I got my blistering self out of there and headed towards the refectory.

With the unexpected inferno coming to life inside me, I had burned through a lot of my energy reserves. I needed to eat. Keeping a lid on my heat was easier when I was well fed.

Lines were already forming by the time I got to the refectory.

Trying to balance my need for fuel with my need to get away before I burned everything within a ten-foot radius, I got in line.

An excruciating five minutes later, I had my metal tray heaped with food—I didn't care what it was—and the five students on either side of me in line were sweating.

A cold wind rushed down from over the wall and ruffled my black hair as I walked onto the green. I let my eyes slide shut and reveled in the coolness. It did nothing to expel the fire inside, but it helped cool the outside of me for at least a few minutes.

Sounds of sizzling ripped my eyes wide open. Glancing down in alarm I realized the sides of my metal tray were red, the food on top scorching. Quickly putting the tray in the grass, it hissed as it hit the moisture in the green blades. I kicked a few stray bits of magic out of the way. One piece caught on the toe of my boot. It was a pretty magenta color—a color I hadn't noticed before.

Expecting it to sizzle up when I touched it, I was surprised when it held its shape and elasticity. Normally I needed to be cooler before I handled the filmy strands. Still pondering why this color didn't mind my temperature, I tugged it from my shoe and put it in the grass beside me. It might come in handy. I'd stuff it into my pocket before I left.

CHAPTER 9

ASPEN

I suffered the lunch line. And then wished I hadn't. My so-called circle of friends would have let me sit with them, but I would have been an object of pity and the butt of naughty jokes. Especially after what happened in history. I refused to tolerate either. With my heart feeling bruised, and the rest of me feeling dejected, I found myself back out on the green.

Looking over, I saw Fire Freak. I still didn't know his name, but he'd helped me today. My middle twinged and I screwed up my courage.

His onyx eyes were large in his face as he saw me coming towards him. It was like he instinctively re-coiled. Uncertainty wavered in my gut, but I was too close to stop now.

I plopped myself down on the grass next to a magenta strand of magic and tried not to be hurt when he scooted a foot or two away from me. I looked down at my tray of dandelion greens and smoked flying fish and swallowed to compose myself.

Clearing my throat, I looked back up at him, nerves jangling. He was staring at me with a look of horror plastered on his face. Ugh. Maybe there were more, uglier rumors spreading about me that were somehow doubly offensive to him? My cheeks blushed and I immediately regulated my temperature to cool them down before their flush could give away my discomfort.

"I...I just wanted to say thank you. For what you did in class today."

His eyes flashed with uncertainty before hardening into black chips of flint. He looked down at his tray in the grass beside him.

"I didn't want to get a frozen splinter in the eye." His voice was full of cold detachment and arrogance. Irritation rushed through me. My eyes narrowed.

"Why are you out here every day?" I asked, trying to keep the annoyance out of my voice.

He gave a mirthless laugh. "Why are you?"

We glared at each other.

"Oh, lookey, lookey! Ice Queen and Fire Freak finally found each other!"

I could have screamed to the highest heavens as Arietta's words grated across me like razor blades. There she was, her red head bobbing next to Kasin's shoulder, the two of them looking at us, lips pursed, unsympathetic amusement written on their faces. Why did they have to be so nasty? I was certain Kasin was feeding Arietta more salacious news. He had no other reason to be with her. He didn't even like her.

A growl sounded deep in the boy's chest next to me.

My eyes landed on the magenta strip of magic between us. A quick twist and I could fake my own disappearance. I knew exactly how I'd knot it up to make myself invisible.

Without another thought, I grabbed the end closest to me and gave it a hard twist.

And careened wildly into a free fall.

A shriek ripped from my lips as a frigid wind encased me.

"What just happened?"

CHAPTER 10

COLE

My hand closed around the resilient piece of bright magic. If I could give it a quick spiral, it might be enough to make me waver into invisibility.

A sharp tug sent me flying backwards and a rushing filled my ears. Someone was screaming and adrenaline sent live flames rippling from my fingertips. I tried to call it back so it wouldn't incinerate the magic to which I desperately clung.

My back cracked as I slammed against hard ground and my flames recalled themselves as the air left me in a *whoosh*. I laid there, gasping for air. I groaned as soon as my lungs opened again. With a twinge, my fire lung opened, and I coughed a puff of black smoke into the air. I had to be bruised all up my spine. My eyes didn't want to work properly—like they were all jiggly in their sockets. Just as I was able to get them focused, I realized my temperature was cooler than normal. And someone was panting heavily to my right.

Jerking my head around, I saw the girl. Pale and sweating, her white-blonde hair was stringing across her neck and shoulders, sticking to her forehead where little droplets beaded. Was I too close? Was she feeling my heat?

But she couldn't be. I hadn't been this cool since...since before Syrai. I shivered. A gentle tug vibrated up my hand. Glancing down, I realized we both held an end of the magenta magic. I let go and watched in horrified fascination as the strand disintegrated into powder that disappeared into the grass. I glanced back up at the girl.

Her eyes were blue like cornflowers edged in ice.

"What just happened?" She croaked as she met my gaze then swung her head around, looking around us. She shook her hair out and in one moment, her color was back to her normal pale-as-cream skin, and the sheen of sweat was gone. The heat began building again in my middle.

Sitting up wrenched another groan from my throat. My back felt like a centaur had clomped all over it. Massaging it with one hand, I propped myself up on my other, not hot enough to scorch the grass yet, and looked around. The walls were still the same. The green was still the same. But something was off.

"There's no magic floating around." I sat up straighter. Where had all the magic gone?

"Look," there was a slight tremor in the girl's voice. She pointed over the side of the wall.

I sucked in a breath between my teeth.

There was no Chasm.

"Where is the island? And the Chasm?" the girl whispered. A river meandered around a mountain where the island and the Chasm should have been.

Flames ran hot under my skin as fear began tickling the base of my aching spine.

Our eyes met, terror clearly working its way across her face.

"What did you do?" she asked.

Was she accusing me?

"What did *I* do?"

"No, I mean what were you trying to do, back...back *home* with the magic?"

"What were *you* trying to do?" I shot back, fear making my voice brittle. I had no desire to admit I was trying to disappear from Arietta. What kind of coward did that?

She glared at me.

She was about to make some retort when a shrill voice cut through the air.

"You two! What in the name of the unicorn are you *doing*?"

In bewilderment, we looked at the plump woman tottering over to us on spindly little goat hooves. She bore a striking resemblance to Ms. Pennywiggle. A younger boy about my own age with pointed ears and dull wide eyes trailed her. They wore clothes that could have come straight out of a medieval painting.

The faun gasped in abject horror when she came up to us, still sprawled and confused in the grass.

"Have you no shame or decency?" The woman nearly shrieked as she looked at the girl's legs, her dark skirt hitting right above her knees. Now that I was looking, she did have great legs.

The girl's eyebrows raised in confusion.

"Excuse me?" She was clearly perplexed. For that matter, so was I.

"Duri! Quickly, your cape!"

The boy fumbled with the clasp on his cape, his eyes never leaving Ice Queen's legs. I flinched as I substituted her nickname in my head even as annoyance with his riveted gaze burned hotter in my gut.

The faun yanked the cape from Duri's sluggish hands and covered the girl's legs.

"For shame!" she practically hissed.

The girl's mouth gaped.

"What are your names? Your actions out here will most certainly be reported to the headmaster!"

My eyebrows shot up. We were being reported for eating lunch on the green? For using a piece of common place magic? Although, glancing around, neither of our trays were anywhere in the vicinity. Was what happened with the magic something forbidden? Dread crept down my neck and spread its fingers over my shoulders. I couldn't leave Magik Prep. Not without learning how to control my flames. The alternative sent my heart to my toes.

The cold seeped off the girl and cooled the side of my arm as her eyes narrowed up at the scandalized faun. "Aspen Frost."

Duri's eyes grew even larger while the faun's cheeks drained of color.

"You get yourself up right this instant, Missy. No kin of Headmaster Frost will disrespect him so blatantly nor so publicly while I am on the premises. And you," she turned to me, "should be ashamed of yourself! What's your name?"

"Cole. Cole Raiden." My voice sounded like churning gravel.

"What is wrong with the two of you? Have you no respect?" the Ms. Pennywiggle doppelganger continued. She bent to snatch my ear, of all things, and I recoiled.

"Stop!" The word strangled in my mouth but before I could jerk far enough away, she clamped her hand around my ear.

Shrieking, she jolted back, cradling her blistered fingers to her chest, and stared at me with fearful eyes.

"I'm sorry! I'm sorry!" Guilt, confusion, and not a small amount of terror roiled through my belly. For a minute I thought I might be sick. Aspen stared at me. Her eyebrows pulled together, but mercifully there was no fear in her gaze. I clung to that as I swallowed down my horror and stood, awkwardly backing up two steps.

"You two march yourselves right into Headmaster Frost's office right this second!" The poor terrorized faun appeared at the end of her capacity. Duri's stupid expression never wavered, but I didn't like the way his eyes kept trailing to Aspen's cape-wrapped legs.

CHAPTER II

ASPEN

My head was reeling as we were marched through familiar stone hallways into the heart of the building. My lungs constricted as we passed places that were similar...but changed...from how they should be. Glass was wavy and bubbled. There were no strands of magic floating around. There were portraits of creatures in medieval dress. The faun and Duri—probably an elf—were dressed like they were going to a Ren Faire. And the reaction to my bared legs. I was in my Academy regulated clothes, for magic's sake!

I glanced at Cole. His mask of indifference had fallen off when the faun had grabbed his ear. He'd been stripped of his protective shell of arrogance, and I'd seen the scared teenager underneath. I could relate to the scared teenager bit. But despite the weirdness going on right now, both in our circumstances and whatever had happened to us, I felt for him. I realized he was an outcast by choice. He feared his own powers.

Before I could ponder that any further, we were ushered into what was the main office—but instead of holding Ms. Pennywiggle's desk, a magic copier, and other random office equipment, the stone walls were yellowish, not darkened with age. Velvet tapestries of a unicorn and a winged lion graced the walls between low shelves full of books and a few baskets, holding who only knew what.

At least the Headmaster's office was in the same place. The heavy brass-bound oaken door stood open, revealing a pale man with a shock of white hair and wooly beard. Hardly daring to believe my eyes, it stopped me like my feet were cemented to the floor.

"Jack Frost?" The words sounded as incredible outside my mouth as they did inside my head. I was staring at a live version of my most famous ancestor. Who had been dead for centuries.

"You were expecting a frost giant?" The wary indignant faun snorted.

The man rose from behind his great mahogany desk.

"Headmaster Frost will do nicely." His voice was deep and rich like hot mulled cider on an icy day. "Mistress Penwig, who are these young people? I do not recall having enrolled any new students."

"Sir, I found them...most indecently...on the green. The girl says her last name is Frost. I would not allow your good name to be sullied, so I brought them straight here. But do be careful of this one." Her fearful eyes turned to Cole who winced. She briefly held up her injured fingers.

My head was spinning. The clothes. The strange familiarity of the building. Jack Frost. It couldn't be. Could it?

I glanced at Cole. His obsidian eyes met me, flashing with sparks of barely contained fire. He was coming to the same conclusion.

"How long has Magik Prep been in operation?" I struggled to get the words out past the boulder of disbelief lodged in my throat.

Jack Frost's bushy white eyebrows drew together in confusion. "Twenty-five years. Why do you ask?"

Twenty-five years? I looked at Cole again. His mouth was parted, his eyes wide, sparks flashing heavily in their black depths. His clenched fingers were red.

The floor spun. I lurched forward and grabbed onto the back of an upholstered chair that immediately stiffened under the frost flowing from my fingertips. My breath came in tight pants, my lungs refusing to cooperate.

We'd gone back in time.

"Mistress Penwig, I think perhaps you and Duri had better leave us."

Without a word the plump faun ushered the sullen boy out the door with her uninjured hand and shut the heavy door behind them.

"Why don't you sit down. Both of you," Jack Frost said, motioning with his hand, his face a mask of concern.

"I can't," Cole said tightly. Glancing back at him by the doorway, he stood rigid, his fists jammed in his pockets, his pulse flapping wildly in his neck up to his chiseled jaw, clenched taut.

"You're Jack Frost." It was all I seemed capable of saying, too gob smacked for anything else.

"And you're clearly a frost fairy," he ventured. His eyes tracked to the chair I'd now covered in ice as my nerves ping ponged around my middle.

An inappropriate giggle worked its way from my throat.

"My dear, are you quite all right? You seem rather distressed."

Cole made a choking noise behind me.

Distressed? Oh, I was way past *distressed*.

Getting a hold of myself, I took a big breath and swallowed.

"We're not from this time," Cole said softly before I could form the words.

Jack Frost came up short, his head jerking painfully. "How is this possible?"

"We don't know," Cole supplied with a swift glance to my face.

Suspicion clouded the older man's face. Before he could deny our claims, my brain started working again.

"You are Jack Frost. One of the founders of Magik Prep Academy. You have two children. A son and a daughter. Your son will have a son. That son will have sons. All the way down the line until one of them named John Frost will have a daughter named Aspen. Aspen Frost." My breath puffed out on my last name, my internal temperature going frigid in my near panic.

"Unbelievable." He stroked his white beard then gave a little chuckle. "Extraordinary. Just extraordinary." A wide smile cracked a line in the middle of his whiskers. He sobered. "But I think perhaps we should take this into my quarters and leave the rest of the school happily oblivious to your presence."

CHAPTER 12

COLE

With my mind reeling, I followed the old white-haired man and Aspen through a tiny corridor at the back of the school. I'd never been in this hall in the present—my mind jolted again as I grappled with the severity of our circumstances.

Aspen's skirt swished softly in front of me. My eyes were drawn again to her legs. Now that I'd noticed them, I couldn't stop looking at them. It was absurd. I'd traveled nearly one thousand years into the past, and all I could think about was the pair of fine legs in the modest skirt, walking down the hall in front of me. I shook my head. Time travel must have warped my brain. There was no other explanation for my wild thoughts about legs that I could never have, let alone touch.

The sunlight was weak behind heavy clouds as we exited the building and made our way across the lawn to a whitewashed stone cottage. With a thatched roof.

A shiver of dread wiggled down my backbone, still tender from the jarring impact earlier. Thatch wasn't good for a guy who couldn't control his internal fire.

Aspen's however-many-greats grandfather quietly unlocked the door with a large brass key from a ring on his belt, and ushered us inside. I ducked my head lower than necessary, afraid my heat would somehow ignite the roof and bring the whole thing crumbling down around our ears. Because we weren't in enough trouble as it was.

"There now. Let's sit down and figure this out, shall we?" Jack said with a friendly smile.

Aspen glanced at me as she sank into a wooden chair at the plank table.

"Would anyone like tea?"

"Tea would be wonderful," Aspen replied.

I nodded, still standing with my hands shoved into my pockets. I was afraid to sit on the furniture. I wasn't sure if time travel would have affected the magic woven into my clothes. Although they were still together in one piece, so maybe they were fine. But that magenta strip had disintegrated. I shivered, thinking what would happen if the magic in my clothes suddenly collapsed. Not only would I be stark naked within seconds as my skin turned my clothes to ash, but the protection they afforded would be gone. All my heat would leach out until I was one big blazing ball of uncontrollable heat.

To be safe, I sunk down against a cool stone wall near the table. Aspen scooted her chair over so I could have a clear view of the table. I nodded at her, still silent.

"I'm your relative, you say?" Jack asked Aspen as he took a kettle off the old-fashioned stove.

"The most famous one in our family line."

"I do hope it's because I did something worthwhile with my life." He poured several mugs of steaming tea.

"You helped found the Academy."

"And the Academy still stands in the future? That's wonderful! We...the hope has always been there." Jack's shoulders sagged in relief, as he sat across the table facing Aspen and me. He said nothing about my sitting on the floor but cocked his head to the side.

Without saying anything, Aspen placed a steaming mug of tea on the floor next to my leg. She briefly met my eyes and some of my brick walls crumbled a little.

"What's the Academy like in the future?" Jack's eyes were practically glowing as he blew a frosty breath on his teacup, dipped a finger in, then took a sip. I heard ice clink against the side of the china.

"In some ways it's very similar," Aspen started. "The structure is largely the same. But there are some pretty drastic differences, too. And I have no idea how your classes or anything operates. That is probably different as well," she hedged, her eyes slowly losing some of the crazed look they'd had in the office.

"To be sure. I'm relieved to know that it survives though." A thoughtful look flitted over his face.

"Do you have reason to worry that it wouldn't?"

He started at my words.

Forehead crinkling, he investigated the rim of his cup. "There are those who oppose all that we've created here."

Aspen sucked in a breath. "The war."

My heart pumped magma through my veins and my eyes were already on her when her gaze flew to mine.

"War?" Jack echoed.

CHAPTER 13

ASPEN

There was no uncertainty in his voice, only resignation. My eyes slit.

"You are not surprised. What have we dropped into the middle of here?" Cole asked, voice strained.

He cleared his throat. "Nothing." He paused. "Yet."

I started to say something, but Jack cut me off.

"I think it would be best if we found out how you got here, and the safest, quickest way to return you to your time. I may ask questions, and desperately want so many answers, but it's probably best if you don't answer anything I ask about the future."

I tucked my lip between my teeth and glanced at Cole as he stood.

"We got here on a piece of magenta magic," he explained.

"Where did you get the magic?" Jack asked.

"In our time, it lays around all over the place. Magic coats every major surface and floats in the hallways. We use it for all kinds of stuff," I said.

"Incredible." Jack stroked his beard.

"You don't have magic like that here." Cole stated the obvious. Black hair slid over his forehead, and he flipped it back with a quick jerk of his head.

"No. You might find the odd string of it up in the towers, but I don't know where else there might be any hiding. And I've never seen any magic colored magenta." He twirled a piece of his beard around his finger. "We do have a number of ancient scrolls and texts in the library. Journals and such. I haven't read all of them, but there may be information there that can help us. Our library has been curated from the very corners of the vast Tri-Kingdoms. You're the only time travelers I've ever met, but surely you can't be the very first? Or the last? If we have any documented resources on time travel, they'll be in the library."

I glanced at Cole. His face was a mask of indifference, though his eyes still held flickering sparks. I was about to ask if we could go to the library right then, but Jack held up his hand.

"I know you must have many questions. And I'll answer any that I can, but I think we can safely assume that we are all as surprised as each other that this has happened. Right now, I have to go. I've got a meeting with Alger-Aodh. I mustn't miss it. And I do feel it would be best if your presence here were kept secret."

Cole's head came up. "Alger-Aodh. The fire-drake?" There was a sense of urgency in his voice that made my belly clench.

"I see his fame precedes him well into the future as well as in the present," Jack said. His eyes shadowed and his lips pursed. He gave his beard a quick tug. "I do not know whether to be concerned or reassured that you both seem well acquainted with aspects of life in my present." He placed his cup in a large basin near the stove. "Please stay here until I return. I think it would be best if your being here were not widely publicized. I will speak with Mistress Penwig and Duri. Your presence, while accidental, could cause some chaos and unnecessary panic among the students. I will accompany my daughter here after her classes finish and introduce her to you then. Please, make yourselves comfortable. You are my guests and welcome in my home."

With another quick nod and a snick of the door, he was gone.

Cole mumbled something that might have been a curse.

"What do we do now?" I whispered, mostly to myself.

"We find a way home. We don't belong here." Cole's voice was also quiet. Almost soft.

His black hair was flopped tiredly over his eyes again. No sparks floated in their inky depths, and his shoulders sagged. He looked as exhausted as I felt.

"I wanted to make myself invisible to them—Arietta and Kasin—when I saw them coming across the green." I don't know if I meant to say it out loud or not, but once it was out, I didn't care if Cole knew. We were stuck back here in the past with no immediate route home. Who was he going to tell?

"Yeah." His one-syllable answer irked me. His hand found the back of his neck. He glanced warily around the cottage, looking longer at the ceiling.

"What's wrong?" I asked when he remained silent.

"Nothing," he sighed. He dropped back onto the floor against the stone wall. "Do you suppose Jack is off telling all the higher ups about us, or do you think he'll keep his own advice and keep us off the radar?"

I tried not to bristle at his semi-insult towards my distant relation. It was a logical question. Although I still didn't like it.

"Innocent until proven guilty?" I asked.

Cole grunted. His belly rumbled.

"I guess we skipped lunch." My own belly growled.

I got up from the table and glanced at the kitchen. It was uncomfortable, poking around someone else's house, but I was hungry, and I was certain Cole was, too. Jack *had* said to make ourselves at home.

In the end, we settled for thick slices of buttered bread.

Little wafts of steam rose from Cole's bread. The bread quickly turned to toast and then charred around the edges where he gingerly held it.

"So, do you think we should stay here until Jack gets back?" I ventured. Cole's neck bobbed slightly as he swallowed the rest of his lunch. For an instant the guard he wore like a suit of armor dropped, and my breath caught as a look of vulnerability swept over him, transforming his face into something beautiful, rather than dark and chilling. But then his eyes hooded, and his mouth pulled taut, and the beauty faded, mask back in place.

He sighed heavily and propped his hands on his knees, careful to keep them away from everything.

"If Professor Rashtin's discussions about the war were accurate, I think it's safe to assume that we're not far off from that time period." He met my gaze. I swallowed. "I'd prefer not to get caught in a war," he said quietly.

I nodded. "Agreed. Particularly one where there's no magic free floating around to use. Ugh. No power weapons. That's a terrifying thought."

Cole nodded.

"I like Jack. I'm probably predisposed to like him because he's an ancestor, but I'd like to abide his wishes if we can. We also have no idea what things are actually like here. I think it might be smart to talk to him more before we go wandering around. Although I'm dying to go exploring." I was itching to explore. I loved history. As much as I wanted to go back to our own time, what an opportunity to see things firsthand!

"You need a longer skirt, for starters." Cole smirked.

I gaped at him before a smile tugged the corner of my mouth.

"Who knew ankles could cause such a ruckus."

"Mistress Penwig knows all about it."

CHAPTER 14

COLE

In the end, we decided to wait for Jack and his daughter to get back, and then to attempt library exploration that night, when the rest of the Academy should be sleeping. Anything to feel proactive about getting back to our own time before an impending war descended. The thought of heading into a large room filled with particularly valuable flammable material did nothing for my anxiety, already ratcheted high with the thatch roof literally looming overhead.

Once we had a plan in place, I retreated into myself and clamped my lips shut, only giving Aspen one- or two-word answers when I had to. I couldn't afford to let her put any more chinks in the walls I'd built around myself. Those walls were what kept people safe from me. I let my eyes linger on her form as she peeked out at the courtyard through the crack in the curtains. Her hair was long and straight, white-blonde. She was lithe like all fae, though it was obvious she was a frost fairy. Everything about her seemed lacy and dainty like the artful scrollwork of a snowflake. Except her eyes. Those I'd seen flash with blue fire. Resisting the urge to let loose a heavy sigh, I did allow myself to admit that she seemed genuinely nice in a way most people weren't. Grounded in herself—something I desperately wanted but seemed to be forever reaching for. She also carried none of the fear of me that she should.

"Since you're not speaking to me, and we'll likely be up half the night hunting for hidden scrolls with instructions covering how to time travel, I'm going to go take a nap." She pinned me with her ice-blue eyes, one eyebrow slightly raised in challenge. I grunted. She rolled her eyes and crossed the room to flop down on a low couch. Her breathing soon evened and I envied her ability to relax so completely.

I would have loved to stretch out and take a quick snooze myself, but I was too jittery. Every so often a surge of heat would rush through me with enough force that my clenched hands shook. At some point I did lay down on the cold stone floor. It was autumn, and the flagstones were cool. They felt good on my back and my heat had a safe place to vent.

I must have dropped off because the next thing I knew, the key was clanking in the lock and the handle turned. Blinking a few times to orient myself, the fear of setting the thatch above me raged through my limbs, swiftly erasing any sleepiness. With a mental shake, I stiffly got to my feet. Aspen yawned and unfolded herself from the couch.

"Hello, I see nothing has happened to call you back to your time," Jack said as he held the door open and a young woman about my age with the same white-blonde hair and light blue eyes as Aspen came through ahead of him.

Her cornflower eyes widened when she saw us. Her hand went to her mouth uncertainly.

"Anna Beth, these are the guests I was telling you about." Jack gently propelled his daughter into the room with a hand to her back.

"Yes, but a part of me thought it couldn't be real," the girl whispered.

"Hi, I'm Aspen."

"Cole," I grunted, voice crackling like burning embers.

"A pleasure, I'm sure," Anna Beth murmured demurely. Her eyes tracked to me, and my muscles grew tight. Unease slithered in between the flames in my gut. There it was. Interest. Silently cursing my fire-drake genes that made me so attractive to females, I tried to paste on a disinterested smile, but it probably looked more like a pained grimace. Flames licked under my skin as agitation rose within me.

"We've brought dinner with us," Jack offered, breaking the mounting tension. "Fresh fish and chips." He held up a large burlap bag.

"Smells delicious." Aspen said. Anna Beth's eyes grew large enough to show the whites around her blue irises as Aspen walked towards the table, her legs visible from the knee down. Aspen cringed.

"Anna Beth, perhaps you could lend Aspen a change of clothes?" Jack asked, careful not to look at Aspen's exposed calves and ankles.

"Sorry." Aspen's cheeks blushed before the pink quickly faded. "It's not considered immodest where—when—we come from." She shrugged helplessly as her cheeks pinked lightly. "It's actually my school uniform."

"You don't say?" Jack said as he averted his eyes and gathered plates from a cupboard above the counter.

Anna Beth must have been properly scandalized, or my fire-drake genes were making her nervous in her attraction, because she beat a hasty retreat to one of two doors in the cottage and was back moments later with a bundle of blue and white cloth.

"Here, I hope these are acceptable." Anna Beth held the bundle out to Aspen.

"Thank you. I'm sure it will be perfect. Where should I change?"

"Oh, here. Please, use my room." Anna Beth motioned to the door, a tentative smile on her face.

Aspen nodded and disappeared into the room Anna Beth had just come from.

"Let's get dinner on the table. Cole, I don't know if this will help, but I scrounged up some magic. I thought it might let you sit at the table?"

Jack was trying to be hospitable, but irrational resentment still flared beneath my skin. I don't know if I was angrier at Jack for being so nonchalant about my condition—not that he understood it, or at myself for my inability to control my condition.

The older man tugged a few strands of filmy green magic from his pocket. They weren't nearly enough.

"Thank you," I said between clenched teeth. "It's still probably safer for me to sit on the floor."

I was spared more awkwardness as Aspen came through the door. Heat rushed to my face as she entered the room. While I missed her long legs in her other skirt, the white ruffly thing she wore on the top was scooped wide and showed her collarbones and part of her shoulders. The full blue skirt dusted the tops of her shoes but was cinched up tight in some sort of medieval bodice that showed off her slender waist and came up right underneath her chest. Quickly, I ducked my head. I didn't need to check out her boobs.

Before I could make a fool of myself staring at her, I turned back to the table, away from Aspen in her medieval allure. Jack had put portions of thick battered fish and golden wedges of fried potatoes onto pewter plates. At least they weren't wooden trenchers. Steam rose into the air and my belly growled. I needed fuel to keep the flames under wraps.

"Shall we eat?" Jack asked. He and Anna Beth sat. Aspen hesitated, looking at me. I scowled at her, grabbed my plate, and slouched to the floor. Aspen's eyebrows rose as she sank into her chair.

"Would you tell us more about the school as it is now?" Aspen asked politely as she broke off a forkful of fish. I popped a gloriously golden potato wedge into my mouth. It was excellent aside from the charred end where my fingers had touched it.

Jack took a drink of his cider and spoke, "As you probably know, there was great opposition to the founding of the school. Many feared what would happen if all the different types of magic were combined in one place. There has never been a safe place for the inclusion of so many different types of magic, or the freedom for so many dissimilar creatures to gather together and learn about each other and our respective magic. In the end, we prevailed, and King Trindon III sanctioned the Academy. Since then, it's been a huge success. We started with just ten students and this castle we renovated. We've raised enrollment every year, and we have some two hundred students and faculty now. It's the biggest it's ever been." Jack smiled proudly.

"But there are still those who don't like it," Aspen said.

Anna Beth quietly took up the story after shyly glancing at me. I let my gaze stay on my dinner, listening, but not making eye contact with anyone. "There are always people who don't like change. And Magik Prep Academy is the first place that has been authorized to allow the inclusion of *any and all* types of magical creatures. The humans have their sanctuaries, but this is ours. Even dangerous creatures are not excluded from the campus, provided all appropriate safety measures are taken and followed to the letter."

Which explained why no one was particularly concerned with my flames. Although I doubt anyone understood the full extent of them. I wondered if I could speak with Alger-Aodh. Jack Frost was to Aspen what Alger-Aodh was to my father's line. If anyone could help me control my wild fire-drake side, it would be him.

And I desperately needed control.

CHAPTER 15

ASPEN

"Do you want me to come with you?" Anna Beth asked hopefully as she handed me a dark cloak later that evening. Not because I would get cold—frost fairies were never bothered by the cold—but it would help me blend into the shadows.

"Thank you, Anna Beth. We'll be all right. We know the layout of the school. That hasn't changed in centuries." I smiled at her. "Besides, who knows how long we'll be. You have classes tomorrow, and I'd feel bad if you fell asleep during them because of us."

"If you're sure," she said softly as her eyes flicked to Cole. I bit the inside of my lip to keep from smiling. Anna Beth was enamored with Cole. Although I wasn't sure why. One evening in his terse company certainly didn't have me falling all over him. But I did have eyes. I knew why she stared at him.

He stood silently, dark eyes glittering in the candlelight, melding into the shadows in his black long-sleeved shirt and black jeans. Even his boots were black.

"Here." Jack started to hand Cole a wooden torch.

"Let Aspen carry it." The words were clipped, as if he expected me to do my fair share. Anna Beth's eyes widened, and her mouth tightened. At last, some common sense from the girl. I took the torch, knowing why Cole needed me to carry it. But he didn't have to sound so high and mighty.

"You should be able to use these green pieces of magic to keep the torch going however long you need." Jack fished them out of his pocket. Shooting a questioning look to Cole, Jack faced me and held them out. I took those, too, while Cole pursed his lips and his eyes hardened.

"Let's go." Cole's words were still short. It rankled me. My skin itched and I wondered if there would be a good time or place to let loose a quick snow shower of irritation. I glanced sideways at my tall, dark companion.

"Thank you," I said to Jack and Anna Beth. "We'll do our best not to wake you when we let ourselves back in."

"Let me know if there's anything else we can do. The inner school should be abandoned by now save the Brownies that comprise the cleaning staff. Everyone else is required to be in their dormitories by sundown on weekdays. Just mind the torch doesn't shine through any windows, or someone will come to investigate. I'd come with you myself, but I have an administrator's meeting shortly. We only ever meet at night to avoid conflicting schedules during the day, and for the benefit of the nocturnal fae. We'll do a patrol of the grounds after, just so you're aware." Jack gave us a fatherly smile and patted my shoulder. I smiled back. He reminded me of my Grandfather Frost from my time. A little pang of homesickness shot through me, and I sighed softly.

Shutting the door carefully behind us, moonlight fell across a strip of grass between the Frosts' cottage and the shadows cast by the enormous stone keep-turned-school.

Neither of us said anything as we silently made our way to the massive double doors that led into the Academy. Without hundreds of years of use, the doors were heavy, but didn't protest as Cole, in a rare show of gentlemanliness, tugged the metal handle open.

I felt the heat coming off the metal as I drifted through and waited for Cole in the darkness of the corridor.

He hesitated.

"You coming?" I jerked my head towards the long dark hallway.

"After you."

I clenched my jaw. Had we not been inside the Academy, I might have frosted his feet to the floor. I bet no one had ever done that to the flaming frustration before.

CHAPTER 16

COLE

Aspen's jaw tightened. I could barely make it out in the moonlight that filtered through the high window set into the stone wall. I hated that I'd made her mad. She'd done nothing wrong. I was a jerk, and I knew it. But better she be angry with me than look at me like Anna Beth did. She was safer that way. I also didn't actually remember where the library was. I knew the general location. It was on the map Ms. Pennywiggle had shown me earlier in the week, but knowing it would only be a fire hazard, I hadn't paid as much attention to it. It wasn't a place I'd normally seek out. Too much potential damage. I was nervous enough about going in there tonight as it was. What if I damaged some text that was crucial to someone somewhere in the hundreds of years between now and when I was supposed to be? Then what? Would we alter the timeline of the world? Did I wield that kind of power? My fingers quaked at the thought. I shoved them into my pockets and shook my head.

With a sigh of longsuffering, Aspen tromped down the hall, the flagstones absorbing her footfalls. I shoved my trembling hands deeper into my pockets and followed her.

The school was eerily still but for a few scuffing noises coming from the hallway that led to the cloisters. I assumed it was the Brownie fae that Jack had warned us about. They were harmless, but the fewer people who knew of our presence, the better.

The library doors were the same heavy brass bound oak as the front doors. I would have opened them for Aspen, one of the few things I could do, but I was afraid I'd super heat it, and the cleaning staff would notice the red-hot metal before it cooled. Plus, if I made Aspen open the door, it would keep my internal walls safe from the destruction I was afraid she had the potential to cause. Those crystalline eyes of hers saw more than I liked.

I could practically feel Aspen roll her eyes as she put the magic and the torch in one hand and yanked on the door with her other. Guilt niggled at me, but I shut it down.

Stepping inside the library was a sweet sort of torture.

I loved to read. Had read all the time before...I closed my eyes against the onslaught of memories and shame that train of thought would bring. Swallowing hard, I inhaled the musty smell of parchment, the sharp, slightly sour smell of walnut ink, the dustiness of leather and vellum. I hadn't stepped foot inside a library in four years.

For four years, I'd been a walking explosion. My hands shook harder inside my pockets, and I clenched them so tight my nails left crescent marks on my palms.

"Cole? You coming? Or am I doing all this solo, too?"

Slowly I opened my eyes and took in the room. Large wavy-paned Gothically-arched windows let in the moonlight. Jack said the windows of the library were magicked so that the sunlight didn't damage the books and scrolls, and that a byproduct of that was that no one could see in through the library windows from the outside. We'd be safe to use the torch in here.

And nobody would see until it was too late if I set the whole room ablaze.

"Coming." My voice rasped. My nerves were strung tighter than a phoenix's tail feathers. And they only came loose once every five years when the burning consumed them. I inhaled. I knew far too much about the consuming burning.

"Any chance you can light this up?" She held up the torch with one of the green strands woven throughout its end. She held it out to me. I swallowed.

"Come on, Flame Boy. You're not going to hurt anything."

My eyebrows raised. Flame Boy? A scathing retort balanced on the tip of my tongue—because that reaction had been my go-to for years—but something in her gaze stopped me. She was annoyed, but she wasn't being nasty. I took a breath as my shoulders bowed under the weight our predicament. She blinked expectantly. I realized with a start that she *needed* me. She *needed* me to work with her to find a way back to our time. No one had *needed* me in years. A different kind of spark lit and swirled lazily inside my gut. It really was exhausting trying to keep her at arm's length. I argued with myself. Not that I'd let her physically any closer than that, but she was right. We needed the torchlight. I could do this. I wasn't going to burn down the school with the lighting of one torch.

"Sure thing, Snowflake." I softened the words with a grin, surprising myself even as my mouth curved upward. Her eyebrow raised but a smile hid in the corner of her mouth. With a jolt, I realized I was teasing her. When was the last time I'd let myself get close enough to tease someone? The bricks in my wall started to crumble perilously. "Unless you prefer Ice Queen?"

"Aspen will do just fine," she replied, her voice a shard of ice. Her eyes lost their hint of sparkle and glinted with something feral.

My heart thudded painfully.

"Should I call you Cole or Fire Freak?" Her eyes were narrowed and with another jolt, I realized her words had found their mark. Despite my walls.

"Whatever," I mumbled, all the fight suddenly leaving me. The weight of the situation suddenly felt suffocating. Grappling with the stress and anxiety of trying not to touch anything anywhere in this foreign place that should be familiar, I didn't see Aspen plant the unlit torch and stalk towards me.

"Why are you such a jerk?" she demanded.

"I have to be a jerk." The words tumbled out without my permission. Her eyebrows flew up her forehead as the moonlight slashed across her face. She was close. Closer than she should be.

Before I could back up a step, she slapped her palm flat on my chest. My nerve endings fired in explosive pulses as fear coated the back of my throat.

"You *don't* have to be a jerk. The world has enough of those."

All the air in the room was suddenly gone. Yanking myself away from her, my body spasmed, flames racing under my skin.

"No, no, no," I whispered like some broken creature as images of Syrai, the last time I'd seen her, floated across my vision.

"Cole. Look at me."

"I'm sorry, I'm so sorry." The words clawed themselves out through the panic welling up inside me alongside the fire.

"Look at me. I'm fine. Shhh. I'm fine." Her voice was kind through the haze of terror pounding through my brain. "I'm sorry I touched you." She held up her hand and the moonlight made her unblemished flesh pale and silvery. My thundering heartbeat halted, and I dragged in a ragged breath.

"I didn't burn you?"

"I'm a frost fairy. I am ice."

"Fire melts. Fire burns. It burns everything." I gripped my chest where my heart still pumped streaks of adrenaline and lava down my veins, albeit closer to its normal rhythm.

"Ice can burn, too." Her words were soft. Drawing in another shuddering breath, I slowly met her gaze, fearful of what I'd find. My internal walls were in shreds.

"You sure I didn't hurt you?"

Her eyes gentled. Not in pity, but in...compassion? Understanding? Could she possibly understand? It all felt foreign. I didn't want pity. Was compassion any better? How could she not pity me? I'd practically come unhinged in front of her a moment ago. I cringed at the recent memory, adrenaline and fear still coursing with the flames inside.

"Cole, I'm fine. Hold your hand out."

"What?"

"Hold up your hand."

I met her eyes again and shook my head as horror stilled my tongue. The look she gave me made me feel stripped bare. The walls I had spent years so carefully constructing did nothing to keep out her clear blue gaze.

Was it possible I could touch her without hurting her?

"Hold out your hand, Cole," she repeated softly.

Without my full consent, my shaking hand rose, dark with suffused fire in the moonlight. When I held it out at chest height, she slowly brought her hand up, too.

"Aspen," I whispered, fear heavy in my voice.

"Your fire can't hurt me, Cole."

Carefully she brought her hand even with mine. My heart thumped painfully against my ribs. I tried to swallow on a desert-dry mouth.

A beautiful river of coolness met my fingers, my palm, my wrist, my arm.

She touched me.

My chest was crushed under the new onslaught of *feeling*. I closed my eyes before the moisture gathering there could steam down onto my cheeks. A fist of emotion lodged in my throat as a harsh gasp escaped my lips.

She didn't move away. Not while I took a breath to try to compose myself. Not while my hand shook. Not while my fire roared inside me.

"Cole, when was the last time someone touched you?"

How was it that this girl could see everything I tried to keep so tightly bound inside me?

"Mistress Penwig touched my ear this afternoon." Mild sarcasm was the best I could do right then.

Aspen frowned. "You know what I mean."

I swallowed and was silent too long.

"Who am I going to tell?" she whispered. It was an invitation to drop the rest of my walls. What was more surprising, was that I wanted to. How long *had* it been since I'd let someone—anyone—this close to me? Literally or figuratively?

"No one but my parents has touched me in four years."

"Four years?" A stunned breath gusted from her. "That's too long." Her fingers shifted and twined between mine.

An ache formed in the cavity where my heart constricted. It *was* too long. And until the moment she'd brought her hand to mine, I hadn't realized how desperately I'd needed to be touched. To feel connected to another being. To feel *seen* as more than an alluring species.

Swallowing, I tried to get ahold of myself, but I couldn't stop my fingers from closing over hers. She was a lifeline, and for just a few moments, I let myself cling to her offered hand. Nothing had ever felt so *good*.

"Are you sure I'm not hurting you?" I whispered. Part of me was terrified that she'd stop touching me, the other half was horrified that I'd leave angry red welts on her perfect skin.

A half smile touched her lips as a tingling shot of *cold* whispered up my arm to my shoulder.

"You act like a jerk to keep everyone away. Not because you *are* a jerk, but because you're afraid of hurting them."

"I'll try to be less of a jerk." The quiet words dropped from my mouth. My fingers squeezed hers ever so lightly, awed at how clearly she saw me.

She smiled fully. "I'll let you know if you're succeeding."

CHAPTER 17

ASPEN

The raw vulnerability on Cole's face tugged painfully at something inside me. I wasn't angry with him anymore. I couldn't be. He was hurt and lonesome. Until recently, I hadn't known what that was like. But after a week of Kasin's rumors, the sly looks from my so-called friends, the giggles behind hands as I passed, and Mykeltie gone on her trip, I had a tiny inkling. But to have to guard yourself like that for four *years*? That was unfathomable. I didn't think I'd have survived it, had it been me.

I brought my hand down, not releasing his. His Adam's apple bobbed as he swallowed hard. He didn't let go of my hand either, his fingers clenched tight around mine. Another wave of compassion washed through me.

"Do you want to go ahead and search in the library tonight?" I wouldn't blame him if he wanted to go collapse somewhere. Even a cyclops could see the emotional turmoil Cole had experienced, and how drained it left him. Just the same, I did feel the need to at least *try* to find something that would help us on our way home. I supposed I could look on my own. I suppressed a shudder. The thought of being alone in the Academy at night sent a little tingle of trepidation down my spine.

"We should. Who knows if we have an expiration date here, or how all this time travel stuff works," he said with a nod, some of his composure returning.

Relief banished the trepidation. Gently tugging his hand over to where I'd propped the torch, I picked it up and held it out to him.

He hesitated, licked his lips, and a bout of heat pulsed against my hand as his fingers twitched. I didn't push him but waited, clasping his hand and trying to offer silent assurance. He needed to do this. Finally, he dragged one finger up and put it against the dry tinder at the top of the torch, and it *whooshed* to life, flames spurting three feet into the air. No wonder he'd needed me to carry it. He'd have incinerated the whole thing on contact. His hand tightened around mine. Painfully tight. He was scared of himself. I squeezed back and sent a cool rush of ice through my fingers to his. Cole pulled in a shuddering breath.

"All right," I said, trying to distract him from himself and make some headway with our impossible task. "If you were a book on time travel, where would you hide?" I held the torch up away from us and the immediate shadows receded.

He sighed. "We'll cover more ground if we split up. I can't touch anything in here without creating an inferno but there's plenty of moonlight over by the windows for me to read spines if they're marked."

"Are you sure?"

"Yeah. My pride is beyond salvageable at this point." He gave a dry chuckle with a slight wince. "I'm trying to be practical at this point."

I smiled at him, the torchlight giving his face a golden glow. The flames reflected in his onyx irises. Squeezing his hand, I nodded.

He held my fingers a moment longer but let go first and trudged towards the massive window. I missed the heat he generated. I was unusual for a frost fairy in that way. I loved the cold as it was in my nature, but I loved the feel of heat against my own iciness.

Cole cleared his throat and turned back towards me. "Aspen?"

"Yeah?"

"Thanks."

"You're welcome." A shiver of heat frissioned through me. "Point number one for not acting like a jerk." I smiled at him.

He snorted. "Right. I'm going to head to the bookcases by the windows."

"I'm going to go up a level and work my way down."

With one last long look at my face, he nodded and turned on his heel.

Scooping up my borrowed skirts so I could move more freely, I held the torch and found the stone staircase. I hadn't realized it was an original feature of the school. I'd been in the library plenty over the years in my own time, but the spiraling stairway to the upper levels was carved out of granite—and for whatever reason, I thought it had been added at a later date, since the rest of the school was made of different stone.

Shrugging it off, I tripped before I even got to the first step. Wretched skirt.

We spent hours poring over books and texts. When the torch started spluttering and my eyes couldn't stay open any longer, I headed down the staircase.

Cole must have heard me because the moonlight flitted off his black hair and I could see his face as he turned to look up at me from the bottom step.

At that second, my foot caught on the long skirt again. My arms pinwheeled, but it was too late. I had two spirals to go before the bottom, but as my body twisted, I felt myself going over the edge of the low carved banister.

The scream died in my throat as I hung on to the torch and plummeted towards the flagstones below.

Arms caught me hard around the middle and my shoulders. The torch tipped, falling against Cole's shoulder and neck. Adrenaline burst through my body, my blood freezing solid.

I did scream then, terrified of what I'd accidentally done to Cole, as the whole torch erupted into flames. Immediately, my reflexes kicked in. I iced the flames to ashes within moments. But Cole!

"Cole?" I could hear the panic in my own voice as I struggled against him. He put me down, quickly stepping back, shoving his hands into his pockets. I followed his retreat, stepping close enough to see his neck where the torch had fallen.

"That was a cool ice trick," he said, voice low and gravelly.

His skin was fine.

"Ooh," I shivered and clutched my arms around my middle. "I thought the torch...when it fell on you..."

"I am fire." He winked as his shoulders lost some of their tension. I felt the barest glimmer of fluttering in my belly. "Just like cold doesn't bother you, flames can't touch me." He shrugged as a weary shadow fell over his face. "My clothes are also pretty heavily magicked. If they can withstand my heat, one torch isn't going to do much." He dusted a sprinkle of frozen ash from his shoulder.

I let out a shuddering sigh. "I'm glad you're not hurt." Relief was a hot rush through my normally frigid body. I was also glad the freeze in my own blood kept my clothes from flaming disintegration. That would have been awkward.

He cocked his head to one side, giving me a curious glance.

"You find anything?" he asked after a second.

"Not much useful. I found some cool books on unicorns and one on the geography around the school. I was curious since there's no Chasm yet. But it was mostly maps of the tri kingdoms. You find anything that looks promising?"

He rubbed the back of his neck and motioned for us to head towards the door. "No. There were a few scrolls that had no outer markings, so I couldn't tell what they were. I wasn't about to touch them, but nothing else. The sections by the windows seem to be mostly about different mythological animals."

"Any species we don't have in our time?"

He gave a sardonic chuckle that had me raising my eyebrow. "No. In fact, there were very few hybrid animals at all that are commonplace in our time. At least judging by the titles."

"I wonder why."

We paused at the door and listened. My shoulder brushed his and he leaned into me slightly. I stifled a grin. Satisfaction that I'd been able to offer help—comfort—to Cole was like a nice drink of hot cocoa settling in my belly. We continued listening. Not that we could hear anything through the thick wood. It was a pointless exercise, but we stood there an extra minute anyway, shoulders pressed against each other.

"You get another not-a-jerk-point if you open the door for me." I glanced up at him. His eyebrows were halfway up his forehead, and his mouth had an amused tilt.

He said nothing but grasped the brass handle. I could feel the heat radiating off the metal. Part of me wanted to step closer to the overheated doorhandle and let that delicious heat seep into my skin.

He cracked the door open, and I popped my head out. The coast was clear. Not a Brownie with a broom in sight.

Stealthily, we made our way back to Jack's cottage as the sky took on the barest shades of grey. My breath puffed in the night. A faint mist rose from Cole's shoulders.

We quietly made our way into the house. I had to smile when I saw two pallets made up on the floor of the living room, one on either side of the wide fireplace.

I was asleep within minutes.

CHAPTER 18

COLE

There were a few clangs from the kitchen area that startled me from sleep, which wasn't all that deep. I would have loved to curl up on the pallet opposite Aspen's, but my clothes didn't cover my neck, face, or hair. Even if I could have tucked my hands into my shirt sleeves, any material that touched my exposed skin was a likely target for incineration. So, I stretched out on the flagstone floor again. It wasn't comfortable, but I was tired enough I didn't care much. My emotions were wrung out like an old dish rag, even though I felt lighter and somehow cleaner than I had in years. The oblivion of sleep was welcome, even if it was fleeting. My body was almost as wrecked as my emotions. My back was still stiff from the fall through time, and for a while it was good to stretch out on the cold stones. I felt differently by midafternoon when I woke up with a crick in my neck.

"Cole? Did you sleep on the floor all night? Er, day?" Aspen croaked from across the room.

I groaned as my aching joints protested as I turned and glanced over at Aspen. She covered a yawn from where she sat on her nice, plump pallet.

"Flammable." I twitched my hands in the air.

"Oh. Sorry. I didn't think of that."

I grimaced. I could think of little else. Although the memory of the *feel* of Aspen's cool touch against my skin quickly surfaced. I needed contact. Wanted it. Wanted it like I wanted air. But had too much pride to ask for it. And I wasn't sure I had enough guts to risk trying to touch her. It had been one thing when she'd fallen off the staircase. While I had enjoyed the aftermath once my heart settled back in my chest, I wasn't sure I should try it again anytime soon. Anyone who got close to me got burned. Maybe not just literally.

She swung her legs over her pallet, the borrowed skirt bunched up by her knees, leaving her legs bare again. I turned my face so I couldn't stare.

"Do you suppose they bathe regularly? I'd commit a small act of treason for a hot shower right now."

"I know what you mean." I could smell myself, and it wasn't pretty.

She heaved herself to her feet and walked towards me. My heart rate picked up.

Reaching a hand down to me, a shy smile curved her lips upwards.

"Come on, Flame Boy. We need to strategize."

Stilling any tremors in my fingers and the cautionary voice in my head, I carefully clasped her hand. Icy cool spread up my arm again. My eyes slid shut for a split second, savoring the feel of both her iciness and being touched. I opened my eyes and found her watching me. She smiled. She knew exactly what she was doing. Or at least what she was trying to do. She was trying to be my friend. But my heart pumped faster than it should have for merely a friendly touch. I shut down that line of thinking. Just because Aspen was the first girl who was *able* to touch me in four years didn't mean my hormones had to go get all out of whack. Interrupting my internal chastisement, she sighed.

"What?" Anxiety tripped in my gut. Was she somehow repulsed by me? Embarrassed? Burdened?

Her cheeks pinked quickly before she swallowed, and they returned to their normal paleness.

"I'm an abnormality among the frost folk. I like the heat. Your skin...it's...it's a nice change from my own temperature."

"Oh." I had no idea what else to say. A few more of those new errant sparks flitted lazily in my middle. I let her help me to my feet, instantly missing the contact when she let go and turned towards the kitchen.

"Looks like Jack and Anna Beth left muffins for us. And a note. They'll be back for dinner. I have no idea what time it is, but I'm guessing we have a couple hours?"

We ate muffins and found a giant wooden tub behind the couch.

"I'm having a thought, Cole," Aspen said, staring at the tub.

"Yeah? A good thought or a bad thought?"

"If I fill this tub with snow, could you melt it?" Her blue eyes twinkled up at me.

"Sure?"

A smile lit her eyes.

"Brilliant. Help me move this into Anna Beth's room."

There were a few bumps and scrapes against the stone walls and the wooden frame of Anna Beth's room, but with my sleeves pulled over my hands, together we wrangled the tub into the center of the room. Aspen quickly filled the tub with snow to the brim. It was fascinating to watch the flakes fall from her fingers. It only took her a minute or two.

"How hot do you like your water?" I asked, ready to plunge my hand into the icy crystals and feel the cool for all of a second before I left steam in my wake.

"Mmmm. Just shy of scalding. Don't worry about overheating it. Even if it boils, I can cool it."

My hand went in and seconds later, the tub was full of steaming water.

Aspen leaned over the tub, the steam wafting into her face, gently moving tendrils of her white-blonde hair. She sighed. "Perfect. Thanks!"

I closed the door behind me, a grin on my face. It felt good to be able to do something for someone else. Even if it was only heating bathwater. It was novel—again, Aspen had needed me. It filled me with a sense of purpose I hadn't felt in...since before Syrai. That thought sobered me. I sat down on the cool floor, back braced against the smooth rocks of the wall. Propping my arms on my knees, I let myself replay everything about the moment we flew through time and landed here—trying to make sense of it. Remember any detail that might help.

She came out a long time later. I'd been sitting in my spot against the wall, hands carefully positioned in the air so I couldn't catch anything on fire. Frustratingly, I hadn't remembered any new details.

Her hair was damp, strands of it falling over her shoulders, bare in the white top of Anna Beth's.

"You want a turn?" she asked as she flicked a drippy piece of hair back over her shoulder.

"Definitely." I would never take a quick shower for granted again.

Aspen bit her lip. "How do we empty the tub?"

"Easy." I wiggled my fingers. "Evaporation is just one stage past boiling."

Once I steamed the rest of the water out and the air was heavy with the damp, I had her fill the tub with ice. Once the door was safely shut and I was alone, I stripped and sat on the ice. Immediately I started sinking as the frigid water grew warm within moments. But the cool still felt good on my muscles. I wanted to tip my head back against the rim of the tub, but it was wood, after all, and I didn't want to risk it. Instead, I washed with the soap shavings Aspen had found and left on a chair near the tub. The water was bubbling around me once I finished. I hopped out, at least smelling better, and quickly washed out my clothes. They stank of smoke, dust, and dirt. Fervently, I hoped the magic in them held at least until we could get back to our own time where I had spares.

Wringing out as much water as I could, I put on my damp clothes and let my skin dry them as I evaporated the remaining water in the tub.

Aspen was at the window when I came out, peeking through a crack in the drawn curtain. A crease formed between her light eyebrows.

"What's wrong?" I asked as I closed Anna Beth's door.

"I don't know. There are students milling around in groups and talking. Nothing looks out of the ordinary, but they're all...tense."

I moved to stand behind her at the window. Not quite touching. Until she leaned back slightly so her shoulders hit my chest. I hoped she couldn't feel how my heart slammed against my ribs.

"Look. See that one?" She pointed. I gulped and tried to focus on something other than the sensation of her against me. Forcing my eyes to where she was pointing, there was an elf. I could see his pointed ears from here. His shoulders were tight, his back hunched slightly. His fingers fidgeted.

"Why are they so nervous?"

"I'd like to know that, too." She let the curtain fall closed. "It looks close to sunset. I can't imagine Jack and Anna Beth will be much longer. Curfew for the students is at sundown. I'd give a year's supply of elixir sauce to know why they're so nervous though."

My stomach growled.

Fortunately, Aspen was right. It was only about fifteen increments before the key jangled in the lock and Jack's white head and Anna Beth's slightly blonder one bobbed through the door.

Jack's face was strained. Anna Beth's eyes were wide and twin spots of color dotted her cheeks.

"What happened?" My words brought Jack's head jerking up like he'd forgotten we were in the room.

"Oh, forgive me. I was distracted. I...it, there was a letter." He sighed like an old man bent under the ravages of time. "The wrong hands opened it and word spread before it could be contained." He ran a hand over his thick beard. "Threats." He cleared his throat. "Threats from Lord Broderick."

"Who is Lord Broderick?" Aspen asked.

"He's the ruler of Dhoria," Anna Beth said.

My eyes scrunched. Dhoria? I glanced at Aspen. She shook her head.

"There is no Dhoria in our time," Aspen said as she took the burlap bag from Jack's weary hands.

"I hope that means he and his descendants have been ousted by then," Jack mumbled. "Dhoria is the fourth kingdom we tried to recruit for the alliance to make the Academy possible. It's been twenty-five years, and still Lord Broderick is against us. Indeed, his hate has only grown with the passage of time," Jack said sadly.

Flames of trepidation snaked up my spine. I felt my neck growing redder with the suffused flare. My hands went into my pockets.

"What did the threats say?" Aspen asked. She pulled out the ham and biscuits from the bag and put them onto the pewter plates Anna Beth handed her. My hands twitched inside my pockets.

If war came while we were trapped here, what would we do? How could I protect Aspen?

The thought jolted me hard enough my teeth clicked together. My eyes swept over her graceful form as terror and wonder welled up inside me, making my flames race all the hotter.

"Threats of invasion. I'm sure it's nothing you all need to worry about. The bigger problem is putting out the fires the threats have stirred. People are concerned. But Broderick has sent his threats for years. He's never done anything about them. He likes to cause panic and fear. This time he's succeeded." Jack scowled and plunked his plate down harder than necessary.

"Papa, it will blow over as it has every other time." Anna Beth put her hand on Jack's arm. He smiled tightly at his daughter and patted her hand.

"I'm sure you're right." He turned to us and motioned for us to sit. I bit back a sigh. Aspen handed me a plate, intentionally grazing my fingers as she did. That calmed me some.

I took my seat against the stone wall. My hands clenched in surprise as Aspen brought her plate and sat next to me on the floor.

"What are you doing?" I asked stupidly.

"I thought you might like company." Her eyes wavered with uncertainty. Another brick fell out of my crumbling walls.

"You don't have to do that. I'm sure the chair is more comfortable."

She shrugged a bare shoulder. My mouth went dry.

Without a word, Jack and Anna Beth joined us on the floor. Anna Beth's skirt brushed against the leg of my pants.

"Why...really, this is unnecessary," I started, a flush of grateful embarrassment crawling up my neck, calming some of the raging fires of terror, but raising new flames of awkward appreciation.

"Nonsense. We should have done this yesterday," Jack said. "Anna Beth, pass the honey?" The issue was closed.

Aspen smiled at me and cut a bite of her ham.

The swirl of emotion inside my chest was intense. No one had ever done something like this for me. No one had ever tried to meet me halfway. I swallowed down the emotion and the lingering fear of the impending war as best I could and tried to look normal as I ate my dinner.

Once night had fallen, Aspen and I again made our way silently through the grass to the school building where we sneaked in like spies and made our way back to the library.

"Here's to better luck tonight," Aspen said as she held a new torch out to me. The moonlight caught on her lips as they quirked up in a grin. Heat rushed through me leaving a tingling trail of awareness and something like confidence in its wake. Without reservation this time, I lightly tapped a finger on the stray wisps of magic woven into the torch's end and watched in satisfaction as the sparks jumped to life but didn't whoosh up three feet into the air like it had last night. Was that the tiniest measure of control? Probably only wishful thinking.

I didn't have time to ponder because as Aspen turned towards the library, she gasped. The torch wavered. Quickly, I wrapped my fingers around hers, holding the torch together so it didn't light the library on fire, and so I didn't incinerate it.

Scanning the room to find the cause for her concern, I nearly dropped her hand, too.

Seated demurely in an overstuffed armchair that hadn't been there last night, sat an old man. He was dressed in black, his hands steepled together, his elbows propped on arms of the chair, his legs crossed. His irises were slit like a cat's. Orange sparks seemed to float inside their obsidian depths.

"Good evening, children." His voice sent shivers up and down my limbs. It was deep and rich and cutting. Apprehension prickled the back of my brain.

Never taking my eyes from the imposing stranger, I briefly squeezed Aspen's hand, and let go the torch. She had a grip on it now, and I nudged her back, angling myself in front of her. Fires blazed in my fingers, ready to spring into plumes of flame.

"Who are you?" My voice was cold and detached, sounding much more calm than the thundering going on inside my chest.

The man's mouth lifted in a half smile, his eyelids hooded.

"I am one who has come to aide you."

"How?" Aspen squeaked behind me.

The man rose. He was a giant. He had to be close to seven feet tall, though it was hard to judge in the library because the ceiling was so high. He held a leather-bound book in his hand.

"This." He held the volume up then bent sideways to place it onto the seat of his chair.

He turned back to us, walking with measured steps until he was only a few feet away.

"You've been given a great gift, little drake. You must learn to harness it."

Stunned into stillness, I watched like it was happening to someone else as he reached a long spindly arm forward. Before I had time to flinch away, he gently placed his thumb on my forehead.

My heart stopped as heat rippled and shivered up and down my body.

I blinked as my heart pumped adrenaline, magma, and blood through my veins once more. He was gone.

"What...who...was that?" Aspen whispered. Her cool palm pressed against my back and my eyes closed as I savored the sensation both of her hand and the coolness that calmed the racing flames the man had stirred.

"I think that may have been Alger-Aodh." Confirmation settled in my chest as I said the words aloud. I desperately wished I could call him back, ask him what he meant, ask him how to control the fires that constantly raged inside me. But he was gone. *Poofed* like a column of smoke.

"Are you all right?" she asked, her hand snaking over my shoulder blade to my arm as she stepped to my side.

I swallowed hard, trying to get a grip on my wild emotions. My forehead tingled where the mighty fire-drake had touched me, and the rest of me was reacting to Aspen's hand on my arm. "I think so," I said. My voice was brittle and raspy.

Aspen's forehead crinkled. "You sure?" She didn't sound convinced. I nodded.

"Well, let's see what he left us." Aspen's fingers left my arm as she walked towards the chair.

CHAPTER 19

ASPEN

My hands shook slightly, still charged with the adrenaline that had coursed through me at the shock of seeing the man—Alger-Aodh?—in the chair. The torch had glittering frost marks where my fingers clamped around it. The heat from Cole's back had soothed some of the tremors, but I wouldn't let him know that. I wanted to help him, let him know he had a friend. Neither of us needed any more complications while we were away from our own time. But I did admit to myself that his presence and his heat made me feel safer. Like I was floundering a little less in this weird time warp we'd stumbled into. That was all. He made me feel safe and less alone. Nothing else. I gave myself a slight shake and adjusted my rising internal temperature as I brought my mind back to the present.

Looking down on the worn burgundy velvet of the cushion, the little book was made of well-used leather, a strap tied across its front.

"Does it say what it is?" Cole asked from behind me. I resisted the natural urge to regulate my temperature again and secretly reveled in the heat emanating from him.

"I think it might be a journal." I looked for a place to put the torch.

"Let's prop it on the stairs. It's not going to hurt the granite," Cole offered, seeing my searching. "Huh, look. It says 'A gift from Alger-Aodh to Magik Prep Academy.' Wow."

"I never noticed that in our time. And that's a good idea." I jabbed the end of the torch into a carved detail of the staircase next to the inscription. Satisfied it would hold, I took the journal and sank to the floor where the torch illuminated well enough and cracked the book open.

The Diary of Jonathan Stormwalker.

My eyes devoured the words scrawled in ancient looping cursive. Cole dropped down beside me, warming my left side where he read over my shoulder.

"Flip the page," Cole whispered urgently.

"Hang on. I'm not as fast as you."

We flipped, browsing page after page, until we came to one about mid-way through the book. We both stilled.

Heat blazed off of Cole even as frost itched at the ends of my fingers. The words leapt off the page and emblazoned themselves on my brain.

I've done it. I've managed to travel not just through the realms but through time. I've successfully com-pleted three trips, each time more difficult than the last. My body hasn't reacted well, and I will not make another attempt.

After dozens of endeavors, what finally worked was using the magic of hybrids. But once I used a particular color, only that color of magic could be used to navigate back to the time I left. Even though I'd successfully used orange magic on the first travel, I used a turquoise strand the second trip. I tried to use an orange strand to send me back home, but alas, for all my efforts, it wasn't until I found another piece of turquoise magic that I was able to send myself home. Once a color has been used, only the same color can be used for the opposite effect.

"We've got to find more magenta magic," I breathed.

"Not to be a complete downer, but we haven't seen *any* magic floating around since we got here," Cole said dryly.

My mouth tugged into a tight line. "Jack said there were usually a few pieces floating in the towers. And he did come up with those green strands that we used for the torch."

Cole nodded. "We need to press him for information about where else it might be lurking. And find Alger-Aodh again."

"Cole, your hair," I interrupted. My mouth hung open as there, before my eyes, his hair seemed to...writhe...and change color.

"My hair?"

My eyes roved over his face. The very ends of his hair had taken on the faintest cast of gold—only at the very ends.

"It's turned golden. On the tips." My eyebrows lifted as the color changing seemed to stop and his hair stopped moving.

"What did Alger-Aodh do to me?"

Anxiety clawed at my belly. Famous fire-drake or no, he better not have done anything to Cole. I'd encase his ancient butt in a wall of ice.

"Do you feel well?" I asked, still unsettled.

"Fine. Maybe better than normal." He shrugged. "Do you want to do anything else in here tonight, or just finish reading the journal?"

I turned my eyes back to the yellowed page, my heart slowing its frantic rhythm since Cole wasn't more concerned about what was happening to him. "Let's read more and make sure we're awake to ask Jack about finding magic before he leaves for the day."

CHAPTER 20

COLE

"Your hair!" Anna Beth said as soon as she came into the living area from her bedroom. Her pale eyes widened, and her hand came to her mouth.

Self-conscious, I ran a hand through my black tangles. We'd only been back inside the cottage a few minutes, spending the rest of the night reading over the back half of the journal. Dawn light whispered outside, lancing a weak stream of sunlight between the crack in the curtains. Anna Beth continued staring at me like I'd grown another head.

Aspen looked between Anna Beth and me, her eyebrows moving towards each other.

Jack came out at that moment, saving me from more torturous scrutiny as the girls swung to face him.

"Papa, look at his hair," Anna Beth murmured. So much for no more scrutiny.

My face heated with suffused flames as every eye in the room trained to me. I didn't like being the center of attention. I purposefully avoided attention whenever possible.

Jack gave a surprised bark. "Got yourself blessed by the great fire-drake, did you? He's the only one I told of your appearance. I shouldn't be surprised he sought you out."

"Blessed?" My voice cracked. Maybe it was one of those things that had faded out of legend along with the majority population of fire-drakes. My dad had never mentioned anything about a drake blessing, and that seemed like the kind of thing he'd pass on—blessing or information, if he'd had either to give.

"Aren't you a fire-drake? Don't you know what it is to be blessed by a patriarch?" Anna Beth said, scandalized censure in her tone. Jack shot her a look.

"I'm only half fire-drake," I said tightly. Irritation rose with a plume of flame in my middle.

Jack's face gentled. "I thought there might be something else mixed with your fire-drake blood, but I didn't want to ask as it might be offensive." Jack gave his daughter another hard look. She had the decency to blush.

"Sorry," she mumbled.

"We don't have many...I'm not sure what the polite term in your time is. We don't have many students with mixed heritage," Jack hedged.

I grunted but offered no other information.

Jack and Anna Beth's eyes were both still wide in surprise at the confirmation that I wasn't all fire-drake. *Monster*, my subconscious chattered. Savagely, I shut the voice down. Unease crept up the back of my neck as I could practically see the wheels and questions tumbling about in their heads. Aspen cleared her throat. Flames of relief simmered under my skin.

"What does it mean to be blessed by a fire-drake?" Aspen asked. She glanced at me, and our eyes met briefly. Hers were luminous and maybe slightly worried? Was she worried about me? The thought sent a warm spiral through me that had nothing to do with the heat I regularly generated.

"It's a blessing that can only be passed from the patriarch of a clan. It's a sort of passing the torch. Though, I must confess, I'm surprised he passed it to you, since you're not, well, from this time. But, Alger-Aodh does get glimpses of the future from time to time. I trust he knows what he's about."

"Wait!" Aspen said as I nearly shouted, "What?"

"He can see the future?" Aspen got out before I could form the words. She looked at me, a mix of fear and hope shining there.

Jack raised his hands in his own defense. "He isn't a seer. He only gets glimpses of things from time to time. He never speaks of it. It's not something one pries into. He'd likely roast anyone who did—even old friends. He does what he does for his own reasons. I would not advise seeking him out to ask him about it yourselves, either." Jack gave us a warning look that I had no intention of heeding.

Alger-Aodh could see the future? He'd given me a blessing—and turned my hair gold? Why? What had he seen? Clearly he'd seen enough to find us in the library and give us Stormwalker's journal. I had to find him. I knew in my bones that he could tell us how to get home.

"Noted," Aspen said. I thought I knew her well enough at this point to hear that inflection in her voice that indicated she wouldn't be following Jack's warning either. "Speaking of the future, we may have found a lead on how to get back to our time. Can you tell us where we might be able to find any kind of stored magic? I think we need to find a piece the same color as we came on. Magenta."

"Where to find magic." Jack stroked his beard as we stood, bleary eyed, next to the table. Anna Beth poured some coffee for each of us and coyly handed me a cup, her eyes seeking mine from beneath her fringe of light-colored lashes. It wasn't lost on me when she purposefully let her fingers touch mine. I flinched away, mostly out of habit, but partly out of surprise, and nearly spilled coffee all over the floor. Anna Beth's cheeks flooded with color, and she quickly turned back to the counter and a loaf of bread. Anxiety curdled in my belly. Quickly, I took a hefty drink of the coffee and turned back to what Jack and Aspen were saying.

"You may try the towers. There are several. I found those green bits in the eastern tower. I've never seen magenta colored magic though." Jack's eyebrows drew together as he absently took a sip of his coffee. Ice clinked against the side of the cup. He must have adjusted the temperature of his drink again. Absently, I wondered why he bothered heating any of his drinks at all.

Glancing at Aspen, she had her hands cradled lovingly around her steaming cup. Some of the tension left my shoulders and I smiled to myself before tuning back into the conversation.

"It's possible there's some in the labyrinth of tunnels under the school."

"What's the best way to access the tunnels in this time? I've been in most of the towers, so I should be able to get there, but I've only been in some of the tunnels. They're off limits in our time," Aspen said as her cheeks heated to a light rosy shade before mellowing to her normal paleness. Brave girl. I smirked.

Jack cleared his throat and raised an eyebrow. "Of course. You can get there a number of ways, but there is an outdoor entrance that will be the safest for you all to use without risk of getting caught. We'll show you tonight."

"Thanks," I said.

Aspen smirked at my verbal gratitude. "Not-a-jerk-point," she whispered under her breath. My lips twitched.

Before long, Jack and Anna Beth were out the door for that day's sessions and Aspen and I were swaying on our feet.

I groaned out loud as I looked at my neat pallet made up in the corner of the room. I missed my bed. More than anything else at that moment, I missed laying down on a soft mattress coated in magic so thick there was no chance I'd set fire to it.

"Floor is pretty bad?"

"Yeah." I rubbed the back of my neck thinking about the crick I'd have when I woke.

The floor was every bit as hard and cold as it had been the day before. I wished I'd had my backpack on when we traveled. At least then I'd have something to rest my head against. My back popped in three different places as I sat up.

"I'm awake. I'm restless. I don't want to wait for dark to start searching again," Aspen said from her pallet as her arm flopped over her face and her fingers twitched.

"Do you think it's safe to venture out before dark?"

"Probably not if we're supposed to keep our where-abouts a secret."

I mumbled an agreement as I stretched my shoulders.

"Do you think they—people—realize we're gone, back home?" Her voice held a sliver of fear. Enough for me to give her my full attention.

"I've been trying not to think about it," I said softly as emotion began churning in my middle.

She sighed. "Yeah. Me too. I haven't been very successful. Although it's been nice to get away from the rumors."

There was a pregnant pause. But just as I was screwing up enough courage to ask her about being the Ice Queen, she rushed on.

"My parents call me every week. What if they call and I'm not there? What if we were erased from our own time?" Aspen whispered.

What if we can't ever get back.

The unspoken words hung in the air between us.

I didn't know what to say. I'd had the same thoughts. They still sent anxiety shooting down my limbs and set fire crackling under my skin. I tried to block them out and put my hands on the cold floor to relieve some heat.

She moved her arm enough to look at me. The tiniest ray of sunlight pushed through the crack in the drapes, and I squinted as it hit me across the face.

"Cole, your hair is still gold at the tips. You think it will stay that way?"

"I don't know. I'm still not sure what a fire-drake's blessing entails, although I probably should. Why? Does it look terrible?" I grinned.

"Actually, it's kinda hot."

Tension pinged between us.

Aspen rolled over, grabbing her pillow and smothering her face with it.

"I did not mean to say that out loud."

A laugh—a genuine laugh—worked its way up from my belly. It shocked me almost as much as her words had. It felt good. *Really good*. To laugh. My heart beat with something foreign and sweet that sent a different sort of fire shooting to my fingers.

CHAPTER 21

ASPEN

Flippin frost bite. I could have swallowed my own tongue! The underside of my pillow froze with my mortification. Cole was laughing. *Laughing*. Although it didn't sound like he was laughing *at* me. Not like Kasin had. Not like my so-called friends had. Still. I groaned into my pillow as embarrassment and the ghost of unpleasant memories coiled in my middle. Cole still chuckled.

Peeking out from underneath my pillow, my breathing hitched as I met Cole's gaze. Amber sparks floated lazily in his obsidian eyes, crinkled at the sides as he smiled wider than I'd ever seen him. Frost flaked from my fingertips where I gripped my pillow even as a wild rush of heat spiked up my middle and felt like a painfully good thaw around my heart.

"It's okay. You can come out from behind the pillow," he teased.

I hid my face again. "Nope. I might die of mortification if I do."

Eventually I crawled out of bed, and we shared some leftover biscuits. With nothing else to do before sundown, we repeated our bathing routine from yesterday. Cole was a gentleman and let me go first again. Her got another not-a-jerk-point for that. But while I was soaking in a tub of cooling suds, I let my mind wander.

I thought about Kasin. How his words had hurt me, and how I felt so isolated as a result. About Cole, how his heart must hurt after being alone for so long. I let the flush steal over my skin as I thought about the way those lazy orange flecks had drifted in his irises as he'd looked at me. And then I sunk under the water when I remembered that I'd told him he looked hot with his newly acquired golden tips. It was a miracle I'd survived at the top of the social ladder as long as I had at Magik Prep. Maybe time traveling had addled my capacity for self-preservation.

Rinsing the rest of the bubbles from my hair, I climbed out and wrapped the towel around me. Unable to stop the thoughts from tumbling in, my belly clenched as I wondered what was going on back in our own time. A wave of homesickness swept over me. I hoped my parents and Mykeltie weren't worried. And I hoped that rumors weren't being blown even farther out of proportion in my absence. Would Kasin use this as a way to drive the final nail into my proverbial coffin? My chest tightened as the stress of the whole situation squeezed my lungs. Tiny pin pricks of ice squeezed out the corners of my eyes.

I flinched as Cole's booted foot tapped gently against the door.

"Aspen? You okay in there? I mean, not that you can't stay in there however long you want, but it's getting close to dinner. Jack and Anna Beth will probably be back soon."

"Oh! Sorry! Yes! I'm coming. Sorry! Give me a sec!"

Ice tears vanished and mortification sent my face flaming again. Obviously, I'd lost track of time and it was much later than I thought. Ugh. I got a what-a-jerk point for being so inconsiderate. I scrabbled for the clothes—they needed to be washed—that I'd left on the chair and jammed my arms into the shirt. I got hung up in the wide sleeve and as a result, crashed into the chair, knocking it over and sending it skidding, the wooden legs shrieking over the stone floor.

"Aspen?"

My fingers trembled with pent up frost.

"I'm fine!" Except that it came out two octaves higher than it should have. I shimmied into the long skirt and whipped my hair out of the way.

"Sorry!" I flung the door open. Cole stood there, hands hanging at his sides. His eyes twinkled as one black eyebrow disappeared under the golden tips of his hair.

"You starting a new fashion trend?"

"What?" My heart kicked up as adrenaline flooded my system. I swallowed, desperately trying to regulate my temperature and keep my cheeks from flushing with color.

He lazily dipped his head towards my shoulder and let his eyes linger, smile hiding at the corner of his mouth.

I glanced down. And saw my bare shoulder. And the length of my bare arm. In my haste, I'd completely missed an arm hole and had wedged one arm out of the wide neck. The sleeve trailed down like a deflated balloon. How could I have missed not getting my arm in a sleeve?

A squeak escaped me as my face flamed and snowflakes fell from my fingertips as I whirled around and shoved my arm back into the despicable sleeve.

Cole laughed behind me. The sound kindled something in my belly that twined with my mortification and refused to let me regulate my temperature enough to cool my heated cheeks.

Stiffly I turned back to face him, red cheeks shining. I clenched my fingers, attempting to staunch the flow of flakes. A few still escaped.

Laughter lit his face like sunshine as his eyes swept over me. I resisted the urge to straighten my skirt or run my hands over my not-quite-tucked-in shirt. My heart stilled as sorrow touched his face and the sunshine melted away.

Mortification forgotten, I closed the gap between us and put my hand on his arm. His face shuttered and the muscles under his shirt sleeve were taut and running warmer than usual.

"Cole? Are you okay?" I asked softly.

"Fine."

Now didn't seem to be the time to remind him of the no-jerk-points.

CHAPTER 22

COLE

I'd teased her. I liked her. Too much. Images of Syrai flooded my brain and the water boiled around me, steam pouring into the room as my skin got too hot with pent up emotion. I dug the heels of my hands into my eyes and heaved a sigh. Making quick work of the rest of my bath, I got dressed, shaking my hands through my hair to detangle some of the waves.

My hair was just long enough to see the changed pieces at the ends. I thought a fire-drake's blessing was a good thing, but anxiety still churned my middle as I looked at my hair. I needed to speak with Alger-Aodh. I needed to forget my attraction to Aspen. I needed to figure out where all the magenta magic was hiding so we could go home. If home was still what we thought it was.

My belly soured and I quickly put my hands into the still-steaming water. For one minute, I let go of the hint of control that I had and let my frustration bloom out in live flames.

The water sputtered and sizzled and was evaporated long before my frustration was spent. I called the flames back. Blessedly, they obeyed. It was rare that I had a safe enough place to let the flames go, and the miniscule purge did help a little as I pulled my hands back.

The front door opened. Anna Beth's skirt swished, and Jack's boots clomped twice before the door clicked shut. Heaving a sigh, I threw my clothes on and with my sleeves pulled over my hands, I righted the tub against the wall. I schooled my features into the blank mask that I wore so well.

Time to brick up that wall again.

"Can we check the library again before we go up to the towers?" I whispered as we were on the path towards the school under the cover of darkness sometime later.

"For Alger-Aodh?" A grin flirted with the corner her mouth.

"Like you were going to leave it alone any more than I was," I retorted.

"Sure. I hope he has more information about how to get home—and I hope he has the answers you want from him, too," she finished softly.

"Me, too," I said so quietly I'm not sure she heard.

We made our way in silence to the library. Aspen opened the door so I wouldn't superheat the handle and we slipped into the moonlit darkness of the library.

There was no one else there.

We searched both levels. No velvet chair. No giant old man fire-drake. Not even a whiff of smoke.

To say I was disheartened was an understatement. I don't know what I was expecting, but I thought after last night, there'd be...something.

"I don't think he's coming tonight," Aspen whispered.

"Yeah."

CHAPTER 23

ASPEN

Disappointment sat heavy on Cole's lips. They pulled down at the corners, his eyebrows furrowed. Truth be told, I was mildly irritated that the fire-drake hadn't shown himself tonight. After leaving us the book, and doing whatever he did to Cole, I somehow thought he'd stick around and make another appearance—offer some more practical instructions. At least let us ask what he'd done to Cole.

"Sorry," I felt compelled to say.

Cole shook his head. "We'd best head for the towers. You'll have to take the lead. I've not been in any of them in our time."

I nodded. The moonlight glinted off my pale skin as I motioned us back to the door.

"You just want me to do the work," I teased quietly.

Cole raised an eyebrow.

"You bet I do," he teased back.

And then he did something so out of character, I nearly tripped. His fingers ghosted over my elbow. I glanced at his fingers as they fell away from my arm then looked to his face.

His eyes were wide as if in horror, his eyebrows scrunched like he was confused.

Before he could jerk back in terror, I smiled tentatively, hopefully letting him know that touching me was okay. At least, within reason. He wasn't a creep like Kasin.

Tingles like tiny wisps of ice shivered over my arms as I pulled the heavy door open and poked my head out. We'd have to cross a good portion of the school to make it to the staircase that would lead us up the closest tower.

Careful to keep our ears open, we snaked down the hallway. There was a large lump ahead in the side of the corridor that had me cocking my head to the side. I couldn't hear anything, but I slowed anyway. The back of my neck prickled.

Suddenly, the lump moved. It startled me bad enough that my feet rooted themselves to the floor.

Hands abruptly yanked me to the side, wedging me into the tiny crack of space behind an arched buttress. Cole pressed me back against the stone wall, hands around my waist, shielding me with his larger form and black clothes that blended us into the shadows as a huge ogre lumbered by, shoving a wide broom across the floor. I shuddered and a wave of heat enveloped me. My eyes slid shut as my fingers frosted against Cole's shirt. That was close. We were close. My body had not been in this much contact with anyone since Kasin...

I shuddered and Cole quickly stepped back.

"Sorry," he whispered. His eyes were stricken. "Did I hurt you?"

"No." Was my voice breathless? I inhaled a shaky breath. "I'm fine." We stared at each other as little shimmers of heat and cold lay trapped between us. "Thank you."

He nodded and checked the hallway. The soft swishing of the ogre's broom had vanished.

"Coast is clear," he whispered back to me. I gave myself a mental shake and we continued to the tiny door at the far end of the hallway.

I flinched as it creaked on its hinges. We edged it open only far enough to slip through. Shutting it behind us, we were left in sudden darkness.

"Um, Cole?" I started, feeling my cheeks heat in the inky blackness of the curving stairwell.

"Yeah?"

"I think I dropped the torch back by the buttress."

"Oh."

We said nothing for a moment. I was ready for the floor to open up and swallow me. I was normally so on top of things—and today I'd been so scattered that I'd mortified myself completely, not once, but twice, in front of Cole, and now this.

"Should we go back for it?" I ventured. The Brownie cleaners might have been only grumpy if we'd disturbed their cleaning...but ogres could be downright nasty. And there was the part where we'd have to disclose who we were. I bit my lip, feelings of inadequacy and embarrassment stomping through me.

CHAPTER 24

COLE

My fingers were still tingling where they'd planted themselves against Aspen's waist, and I knew that later I'd be reliving the way she felt pressed against me.

My hands twitched in the darkness. I had an idea, but I wasn't sure it was a good one.

"Aspen, is there anything remotely flammable in the stairwell?"

"Not in our time."

I frowned. What if they had a tapestry or something hanging on a wall?

"Cole?"

A sigh gusted from my lips. This was a risk. A big risk. But maybe...just maybe...I could do this one thing.

"I think I can light a fireball in my hand, but I'm afraid it will be too big and if there's anything that can catch fire in here, that'll be the end of it."

"Ice, remember? I can put a fire out as quickly as you can start it."

I still wasn't convinced.

"Can you try to freeze my arm as I try to light the fire?"

"Like, even out your heat so only a tiny bit gets out?"

"Yeah. Like lighting matches instead of bonfires."

"That shouldn't be a problem. Where are you?"

She moved and her hip connected with mine and sent a tremor rocking through my middle. I needed to get a grip.

"Sorry. Found you. Do you want me to freeze the arm you're going to set on fire, or hold your other hand and try to ice things down from there?"

"Try my arm first. Not that you don't have mad snow skills, but I don't trust my own ability not to shoot flames through the ceiling."

"You can do this, Cole," she said softly. Her words sent a rush of white heat through my middle. The kind that ignited something new inside me. Her hand found my arm. I swallowed as her touch instantly brought cool relief rushing down my arm to my fingers. I didn't know if her touch or her ice felt better. I didn't dwell on it.

"Ready?" I rasped.

"Whenever you are, Flame Boy."

"Funny. Ice it a little more if you can."

"I could turn your arm into a popsicle if I wanted to," she teased.

"No, I don't think you could. Volcanos still melt glaciers," I warned, still uneasy with what I was about to do, but loving the icy cool and her fingers against my arm.

"Yeah, but glaciers don't have inexhaustible sources of freeze." She squeezed my arm and a rush of freezing pin pricks scattered over the surface of my arm down to my fingers while the middle of my arm rushed with pent up heat. I swallowed again and gathered my courage. Imagining a gas light and letting the tiniest trickle of igniter through the crack of an opening, I let my fire go.

To my wild delight, little flames, no longer than my own fingers spurted from the ends of each digit.

"Wow!" Aspen breathed.

My heart pounded, still scared I'd burn things too hot too fast and raze the Academy down. Flexing my fingers together, the flames met in my palm and hovered there, making a palm-sized fireball that showed the small confines of the base of a tall spiral staircase blessedly made of stone. No tapestries in sight.

"Want me to let go now?" Aspen asked, her fingers still cold against the inferno under my skin.

I shook my head. Swallowing hard, I did my best to take full control of the flames in my fingers.

"Okay. You can let go, but slowly." There was a slight tremor in my voice.

Slowly, Aspen's cool rescinded. My flames stayed where they were, until her fingers slid off my arm. Fire whooshed into the stone antechamber.

Cold engulfed my back and spread down my arms. The fires cooled.

"Maybe this isn't such a good idea." My voice trembled as my heart pounded, terror of myself hovering over me like a second skin, waiting to ignite and burn everything I touched. Sweat steamed from my forehead.

"No. You're going to do absolutely fine," Aspen insisted. Her hands trailed over my shoulder and down my arm, keeping her icy presence constant, but stirring things in my gut and raising painful bittersweet emotions that were better left undisturbed.

Half an age later, her cold hand clasped around my hot one—the one not clenched around the fire in my fingertips—and her river of cool lifted from my shoulders, but still flowed through my arm.

"Try again," she urged.

I didn't want to. I wanted to go back for the torch. Aspen squeezed my hand and a sharper freeze trailed up my arm and over my shoulders. Letting her confidence in me boost my courage, I blinked twice in the darkness. Cautiously, I uncurled my fingers a fraction of an inch. The fire plumed three inches above my fingers and stayed as I wanted. Letting out another shaking sigh, I let the fire rest in my palm again.

"Cole, your forehead is gold where Alger-Aodh touched you."

"Gold?"

"Yeah. Seriously. You have a little golden thumb print right in the middle of your head." Her other hand reached up and brushed the fire-drake's mark. The breath froze in my lungs.

"Awesome. I've always wanted a golden tattoo of a thumb print right between my eyes," I grumbled, trying not to be so aware of her.

"It hasn't been there since you got it. Maybe using your fire activates it? Maybe it will fade again."

"I've already got weird hair. Who knows what other surprises are waiting in this time?"

"It could be worse. He could have turned you purple or something." I could hear the smile in her voice as we started up the long stone spiral, my handful of flames behaving themselves and casting flickering shadows against the stones.

Cole's fireball was pretty amazing.

CHAPTER 25

ASPEN

Cole's fireball was pretty amazing. I admired the way the flames danced in his open hand. It was insanely awesome. I could produce an ice globe, snow, hail, icy winds, frost, but to hold fire in my palm? That was something I could never do. And a large part of me found it attractive.

Cole's other hand was gripped around mine like a vice. His terror came through his trembling fingers.

"Look!" he suddenly said, stopping abruptly on the stone stairs. "Is that? Right there." Cole gestured up a few stairs.

Gasping, I would have lunged forward, but Cole's hand tightened on mine. "Sorry. I won't let go. But you're right. That's a strand of magic." I eyed it greedily, not taking my gaze from it as we made our way up the steps to where a spindly bit of green magic hung suspended, snagged on a protruding stone.

Reverently, I reached out and took it down, careful to keep ice flowing from my other hand, still firmly ensconced in Cole's heated grip. The filmy length of it shimmered in the light emanating from Cole's fingers. It was weak, but it was the first strand of it we'd seen aside from the ones Jack had brought back that first day. I'd never take the hordes of floating magic for granted again if we ever got back to our own time.

"It's green." Cole stated the obvious. I was disappointed by this, too.

"But at least we found some." I shrugged. "I guess we keep looking?"

Cole had a pensive expression on his face, the flames creating dark shadows under his angled jaw and to the side of his straight nose. "I wonder if there's a way to change the color of magic? Have you ever heard of doing that?"

My lips pursed. "Well, I've never *heard* of it being done. It's not something that's taught in any of the lower-level magic courses, and if it were a common thing, I'd expect Magik Prep to include it in Magic Wielding 101." I paused. "I don't actually know where the different colored magic comes from, now that I'm thinking about it."

"I don't either. And I've had quite a few different magic courses between the schools I've been to. I've always been taught to use the colors interchangeably, but that was always in a contained environment. Before coming to Magik Prep, I'd never seen so much magic all at once. At my other schools it was always carefully monitored. It wasn't like they couldn't get more, but it wasn't floating down the hallways either."

"I've always heard it's built up over time. And since there's next to none here, I guess that's true? It hasn't been here long enough to accrue?" I tucked the strand of magic into the pocket of my borrowed skirt and nodded to the stairwell. "Shall we see what's farther up?"

He squeezed my hand and we continued up the stairs. We searched every nook and cranny we could find for hidden bits of magic. It took a lot longer than I expected, partly because we were being so thorough in our search, and partly because Cole was afraid to let his flames get much higher, so we had limited light to work with and that delayed a quicker search. I didn't mind too much though. We held hands the entire time. And he gave me a sense of safety in a world gone crazy, warped through the reverse passage of time.

Though my heart was still wary of romance after Kasin, I was drawn to Cole in a way I'd never been to anyone else. Traveling back centuries in time had done something to us that bonded us together. We'd spent nearly every waking hour together for the past few days and had gotten to know each other surprisingly well. While I still didn't know his favorite color, I knew his deepest fears. I didn't know his favorite food, but I knew he'd closed himself off from the world to keep the world safe from his flames.

A loud gurgle drew me from my reverie.

"Was that your stomach?" I glanced at his belly, safely tucked away under his magicked shirt.

"Yeah. Sorry. Keeping my flames up has burned through all my energy. I'm starving."

Guilt nudged me. It was my fault we didn't have the torch.

"Sorry I left the torch."

"That's okay." There was a hidden heat in his words that tickled my belly. Did his hand just get warmer against mine? "Hey, look!" He pointed his cupped flames to the top of the stairs.

The faintest traces of grey light appeared at the end of the last spiral. Speeding up, we came up onto the landing of the uppermost part of the tower. We were in a large circular room that had several open floor-to-ceiling windows. A cold breeze blew in from the outside, swirling around us like a mini cyclone. I shivered and adjusted my temperature cooler to match.

"Wow." Cole brought us to the center of the room, and we looked around. The stars twinkled and a strip of grey sky met the mountain in the distance where the Chasm should have been.

"It's later than I thought," I murmured, suddenly tired. I resisted the urge to lean against Cole's arm.

"Yeah. If that's dawn coming, then we need to be back at Jack's soon."

"You need to eat, too. It's light enough. You can let the flames go."

"I probably should. They'll be visible quite a distance from up here."

I eased back my ice, reluctant to let go of his hand. His fingers twitched around mine, keeping my hand in his as he curled his fingers in, the flames shrinking.

"I miss the sun," I whispered as we stood there, unmoving in the near-dark as the first shadows appeared on the lawn and the stars began to twinkle out. It felt like an eternity since I'd felt its heat on my face.

"So, let's watch a sunrise. At least part of one. We should still have enough time to make it back before people are up and about."

Glancing up at him, he turned so I could see his face. His eyes were trained on me. Amber flecks were lazily going up and down in them again. My lips curved up.

"You get a lot of not-a-jerk points for that." I turned my face back to the window. The faintest edges of light crept over the far side of the plain beside the mountain, casting the meadow lands in a dazzling wash of orange and yellow.

"We might as well sit." Cole slowly released my hand and sat on the floor. Soft shadows cupped his eyes in the grey light. He was all shades of white and black except his eyes. They still glowed with little flecks.

I missed his hand. More than I cared to admit. My skirt *poofed* around me as I sat close to him.

Another chill wind blew in through the windows and I shivered, not bothered by the cold, but missing Cole's heat. Glancing sideways at Cole, I bit my lip. And decided to be impulsive.

CHAPTER 26

COLE

The tower was cold, the wind almost punishing, and the floor beneath me nearly freezing. It was awesome—a welcome relief from the constant swelter of my own heat. I let the breeze wash over me, taking some lingering tension from holding my flames steady for so long. My stomach grumbled again, but I ignored it. For the first time, my flames felt content. With help, I'd held them steady for hours. Which was more than I'd been able to accomplish otherwise in the past four years. Maybe the constant use had burned off enough energy that I wouldn't set anything on fire in the next few minutes.

Aspen shifted beside me. I longed to reach out and put my arm around her, but that wouldn't be wise. That was territory I couldn't enter. A dull ache began in my chest. I stretched my legs out in front of me as the sun burst over the horizon in a crescendo of yellows, oranges, and hot pink that streaked the sky like beautiful flames. Flames that wouldn't incinerate everything they touched. I flinched at the thought. Shadows fled under the mighty reign of the sun. Would that it could move the shadows from my insides. So much hurt and anguish still remained, all tied up in knots. Knots I was afraid I'd never be able to undo.

"Move over. Just because the cold doesn't bother me doesn't mean I don't like to feel the heat." Aspen scooted right over the top of my extended leg and planted herself on the stone floor between my legs.

I was shocked speechless. She leaned her back against my chest, and I swallowed hard as my pulse careened through me.

She sighed in contentment. "The perfect temperature."

Did she have no idea what she was doing to me? I swallowed thickly again, trying desperately not to think about Aspen practically sitting on my lap. Without my permission, my hands found her arms, cradling them as my heat enveloped us both.

Her ear, pointed and so delicate it was nearly translucent in the early morning light, was inches from my face. She leaned her head back against my shoulder, seemingly perfectly at ease. Her neck was long and white. My heart rate picked up even more as my temperature began to rise. This wasn't wise. This wasn't safe. I was going to combust and go supernova right here on the top of the eastern tower of the Academy.

What would her neck taste like? Would she let me put my lips on it? Could I put my lips on it? I shouldn't. I absolutely shouldn't. Flames erupted underneath my skin.

"Cole, you're getting hot."

"What?" Jerking, I shoved her away from me. "Sorry! Sorry. Are you all right? Did I burn you?" My heart thumped hard against my ribs. Even after feeling her ice travel up my arm most of the night, part of me feared she'd gone through her reserves and my heat would scorch her. Fear of myself and what I might have done to her lingered even as I searched her for scorch marks.

She turned her icy blue eyes to my face. "Cole. I'm fine. You can't hurt me. Here." She held her hand out, pale and unmarked. Trembling, I lifted my own hand, long fingered and red with pent up heat. Aspen gently touched her palm to mine, her ice to my fire. A cold wave of relief spread from my hand to my arm. The heat fell away leaving a tingling awareness in its place.

"You've been using your ice all night. I was afraid maybe you'd come to the end of it, and I burned you," I whispered.

"I think my ice is like your heat. It's always present. I don't think I *can* run out." She smiled softly.

"I'd like to run out of heat. It would be nice not to constantly worry about incineration," I said dryly.

She scrunched her face in sympathy, but then turned and scooted back up against me. It did nothing to help calm the raging flames under my skin, and it did wonders to fan the other flames that were blazing to life even though I tried to tamp them down. It felt so good to touch someone. To touch *her*. To feel her trust tangibly in a way I hadn't felt anything in years.

"I told you I missed the sun. What's one thing you miss from our time?"

Against my better judgement, I leaned my chin against the top of her head, my hands finding her arms again. I closed my eyes and inhaled. I shouldn't have. She smelled like honey and sweet fresh snowfall. "Ice cream." My voice hitched.

"Mmm. What's your favorite flavor?"

"I'm not particular." I cleared my throat and went for another not-a-jerk point. "Ice cream only stays cool for a second or two for me, but it's the best sensation when you're a walking inferno. The second that freezing cold ice cream is on my tongue before it melts is amazing."

Aspen cleared her throat and her hands clenched together like she was uncomfortable. I almost asked her what was wrong, but she spoke again before I could.

"I like chocolate with cherries."

"Sounds good."

She sat straight up. "Cole. Let's make ice cream tonight!"

"Don't we need to find more magic?"

"Yes. But I think trying times call for creative stress relief, too. My nerves are so brittle with all this mess hanging over us, I think I might snap in two. I bet we could figure out a general ice cream recipe. You heat it and then I'll freeze it. I am the Queen of Ice."

The words died on her tongue as her words mimicked the rumors that had surrounded her. My chest tightened in response. The sudden thought of the tool doing anything with or to Aspen sent my blood rushing dangerously hot. She sighed heavily and wouldn't meet my eyes.

"Do you think we could sneak into the kitchens after hours?" I ignored the invitation to ask her about the rumors, though I almost wished I hadn't.

Relief sagged her shoulders. "I think we can. Come on. We'd better get going before we can't without being seen and give Jack more white hair."

The sun was blazing up the side of the mountain now. We needed to hurry.

CHAPTER 27

ASPEN

I'm the Queen of Ice? How could those words have slipped between my lips? It was true. I was the Queen of Ice...but I resented the words after Kasin twisted them against me. I knew Cole had heard the rumors by the way his body tensed and his heat kicked up another notch. I wanted to melt away in mortification. It bothered me so much more now than it would have before we'd traveled back to the time of our ancestors. Because I cared what he thought of me now. Because I cared about him. Modulating my temperature to keep my cheeks from blushing, I paused to look once more out the window at the glorious ball of color rising in the distance.

With a sigh I crept back down the stairs into the darkness.

"Are you okay to keep going? I can see hardly anything. Do you want the flames again?" Cole asked from somewhere behind me.

It was pretty dark. I was feeling my way down with my hand against the rough stone.

"Maybe until we get to the main level?"

Cole came even with me on the step. A shiver worked its way down my spine when his hot fingers clasped around my frigid ones.

"Ready?" he asked.

I sent a wave of cold up his arm and a neat little fire ball plumed to life in his opposite hand.

"Perfect." It was. He'd made a brilliant *little* sphere of fire.

"The ice helps," he confessed.

We moved down and crept to the door of the stair-well. Cole extinguished his flames as his belly rumbled once more. Poking my head out, I did a quick scan, then we scurried like mice chased by a cat through the hall and all the way to the cottage.

"Bless me, I was afraid you'd vanished!" Jack said, hand clutching at the buttons over his chest as we came in and quickly shut the door behind us.

"Sorry. We were up in one of the towers. We found a piece of green magic, but no magenta." I took a big breath to still my heart that was still racing.

"Cole! What happened to your hair?" Anna Beth cried as she exited her bedroom and came towards us. My eyes swung around, not having noticed anything unusual.

"Oh." It dropped gracelessly from my lips.

"It's so...unusual," Anna Beth ventured. Her eyes were big in her pale face. She made as if to reach out and touch Cole's hair, but he jerked back. I silently willed the shards of ice that raised like hackles inside me to melt back to where they belonged. Was that *jealousy* that frosted over my insides?

"What's wrong with it?" He tugged a piece down over his forehead. "Did it change colors again?"

"Kind of," I offered. I resisted to urge to run my fingers over it like Anna Beth had tried to do. I thought he'd let me touch him, but just because *I* wanted to, didn't mean *he'd* want me to. And it would be incredibly rude to do it in front of Anna Beth. Even though I kind of wanted to let her know that Cole was absolutely off limits to her. Not that I had a proper claim. Blinking, I glanced back at Cole's hair. "It's got a hint of bronze behind the gold, then the rest of it is still black."

"Is the thumb print still visible?"

"The fire-drake's blessing?" Jack chimed, watching us with avid interest from the kitchen.

"Mm hmm," Cole mumbled as he flipped his hair off his forehead and turned towards me. Anna Beth's mouth turned down slightly at the corners.

"I can't see it at all now," I said, squinting at the place the golden thumb print had last been visible.

"Does it...activate?" Cole turned his question to Jack. Anna Beth moved stiffly to put tea into the pot on the stove.

"I honestly don't know." Jack shrugged his shoulders. "I can try to get a message to Alger-Aodh today if you like though."

"Would you, please?" The longing in Cole's voice was enough that Anna Beth glanced up at him from the stove.

"I'll do my best. But know that if the fire-drake doesn't want to be found, he won't be."

Cole's stomach growled.

"Sorry. Any chance of breakfast?" Cole winced.

"Here you go," Anna Beth said primly. She opened the oven and pulled out two plates of bacon, eggs, and biscuits slathered in gravy on the table. His eyes widened in appreciation even as my stomach twisted in anticipation.

"Thanks," he said, carefully taking a plate without touching the table.

She nodded curtly. "We already ate."

"Aspen," Jack's voice was suddenly serious.

Anxiety cramped my belly as a bite of eggs slid down my throat.

"What?" The word strangled from my mouth.

"Look!" Jack carefully touched my sleeve where, hidden in a crease of the voluminous material, a few tiny specks of magenta dust had gathered.

I gasped.

"Cole, look," I murmured, half in shock.

"Is that magic?" he asked incredulously.

"It looks like it could be," Jack commented. I held perfectly still as he snatched an empty plate and cautiously swept the tiny flecks onto the shiny surface.

"It's the right color. How do we make a strand of it?" Cole asked.

"Unfortunately, I don't know the answer to that, either," Jack said. "I've never seen this color before. But it's here now. Do what you can with it. We've got to go, or we'll arouse unnecessary suspicions with our tardiness. Do you need anything else today? There's more food in the pantry."

"We'll be fine. Thank you, Jack. For everything. You, too, Anna Beth." My words were sincere, even though my ice claws had wanted to take a swipe at Anna Beth just moments before. Finding even the specks of magenta magic had a softening effect on me. Though I didn't expect we'd be able to manipulate the magic dust into anything usable, a small part of me was hopeful.

Once we were alone, we sat on the floor, breakfast on our laps, the plate of tiny magic crystals between us.

"I think this is what we're looking for. But, even if we can find a way to make it into a strand big enough we can both twist together, I don't think this is enough." I frowned at the plate of pinkish smudges.

"I agree." Cole sighed. "So, I guess the question is where did we pick this up?"

"It had to be somewhere between here and the tower. Although, with all the wind in the tower, I'd have expected it to blow this off me. Maybe we picked it up somewhere in the stairwell?"

"Maybe that's why there isn't any magic high up in the tower. Maybe the wind blows it all out before it can stick."

"Oh, I hadn't thought of that." My finger tapped my lip. "I keep thinking about the Chasm. How Professor Rashtin said there was a glacier that the great fire-drake melted to form the island."

"Alger-Aodh. He's the most infamous fire-drake in the history of fire-drakes, and he's here. Jack said he can glimpse the future. I'd give my right arm to talk to him about what's coming. And how to get home."

"I know what you mean. What if Alger-Aodh somehow used, er uses, magic that blew out of the tower to defeat Lord Broderick's forces—since we know there's at least some magic there. We found the green strand and then the dust. What if that magic is blowing out and getting caught somewhere near the river? And somehow that's what Alger-Aodh manipulates into forming the island and the Chasm?"

"Wow, Aspen. That's...that's an impressive leap." Cole's brows drew down as his long fingers tapped against the stone floor. "But that makes sense. I mean, only based on what I've learned to do with magic in our own time, that could be a possible outcome. Someone as old and theoretically experienced with magic as Alger-Aodh should have no trouble with that at all."

Heat scuttled through me as he looked at me appreciatively, a new respect lighting his eyes. "What if we make that ice cream tonight and search another tower; go sleep for a few hours, then sneak out to the river during daylight? I'm not sure I want to venture that far outside the Academy walls after dark." I bit my lip.

"You sure you want to stop the search long enough to make ice cream?" he asked me, no judgment in his tone.

I sighed, feeling the stress of our situation in my bones. I was enjoying my time here away from Kasin and his rumors, despite the things we knew were coming, but I also ached for home. For the familiar. "I need ice cream. I need something comforting from our own time."

"I can appreciate that. I'm not going to turn down ice cream if there's any to be had. I also agree it would be smarter to go to the river during the day. I'd say let's go right now but using my fire all night has taken more out of me than I think I realized."

Even as he said it, his eyelids began to droop. I was bone weary, too. We both needed rest.

"That works for me." Yawning, I covered my mouth with the back of my hand.

"Good night, Aspen." His quiet words brought a flush to my face for no reason. His black eyes had tiny amber motes floating in them again as they slid shut. His breathing evened out almost immediately, propped there against the wall.

"Night, Cole," I whispered.

CHAPTER 28

COLE

Hours later, my back popped four times in quick succession, my body protesting being motionless for too long. I'd slept hard. Despite the stone floor and the discomfort it caused, I felt more rested than I had in weeks.

Aspen's breathing was still even, so I just laid there, letting my mind spin.

Unbidden, Syrai sped through my brain. I winced, and couldn't help the comparisons I drew, thinking of Aspen and Syrai. Syrai had been so long ago, but the terror was still fresh. Terror that clouded what I felt, and what I wanted to feel, for Aspen.

Jack had some news for us that night at dinner. We all sat again on the floor with our plates of roast chicken and potatoes and a side of something that looked suspiciously like skinny entrails. I tried not to look too closely.

"I went up in the tower today after you found that magic dust. I wanted to take a look for myself. I didn't see any more of the dust, but I did see the slightest flash of something that looked like magic out by the river. I was looking out the tower window, and I caught whatever it was only in my periphery, but it was there. I would have gone right out to the river after that, but duties prevented it. I'd suggest it's significant enough to warrant a closer look." He stabbed at a potato as it rolled towards the edge of his plate.

Catching Aspen's gaze, her eyes were lit with blue fires of excitement that matched my own. Maybe there *was* magic blowing out of the tower and getting caught somewhere by the river. Just waiting for us to find it and use it to get back to our own time.

"We were thinking about searching there tomorrow afternoon," Aspen said.

Jack nodded. "I think it would be worth your time."

"Do you think it will work? Even if you find the color of magic you need, will you be able to go back to your own time?" Anna Beth asked, her face inscrutable.

"It has to," Aspen said quietly, giving Anna Beth a puzzling sympathetic look. Anna Beth glanced at me then back to her plate.

Once the school was asleep, Aspen and I snuck out the cottage door. I was beginning to feel like a spy from some thriller story, except that we never seemed to get any closer to attaining our goal. We were on an endless loop. Go out. Search. Find nothing. No explosions, no rescuing the girl, no goal attained.

Although, stealing a quick look at Aspen made my heart kick up a notch. I wanted the girl. Wanted to be the hero. Wanted to insert myself into her world of ice more than I'd wanted anything in a long time. Unfortunately, that was not the sort of story we were in. I was no hero, and I had no way of saving Aspen from this time and getting her back to our own. Had no way to protect her from the battle we knew was coming. I suppressed a sigh. If Alger-Aodh ever chose to show his face again, maybe I could forsake my pride and ask if there was a way to change my story.

The kitchens were past the cloisters, down a long hallway, and jutted off to the side in their own separate building attached to the rest of the school. It looked like a new addition to the already-ancient stone castle that housed the Academy proper. The founders must have remodeled this part. The refectory was still in the same spot as in our time, although it was significantly larger in present day, and had undergone plenty of improvements over the ages.

We slipped in the doors of the yellow stone building, the scents of herbs and smoked meat meeting us as the door snicked shut behind us.

Aspen took a deep lungful. "It's a literal medieval kitchen. I studied this sort of thing freshman year. This is incredible. To think I'm actually standing in one." Her face was slightly perplexed, partly in awe of our surroundings.

And I suppose, from an historical point of view, it was pretty fantastic. Large windows high up in the walls let in streams of moonlight. A huge granite countertop ran halfway around the whole back part of the room. It was the same type of granite that the stairs in the library were made from. They must have been quarried from the same place. Three massive tubs were lined against the wall. Near the tubs was an old-fashioned hand pump.

"Huh," Aspen murmured. "Indoor plumbing." She nodded to the pump.

A great trestle table filled the middle of the room and an assortment of fruit, vegetables, and rounds of bread sat out in crockery bowls. Shiny copper pans, pots, and kettles hung from a rack in the ceiling.

"If I were fresh cream, sugar, and eggs, where would I hide?" Aspen glanced around.

"Eggs are in a bowl on the table," I offered.

"*Mrooo*!"

Aspen clutched her chest as fire raged through my arms.

"Flipping frostbite. Was...was that a *cow*?" Aspen gasped. Her eyes were huge in her face, the moonlight illuminating the whites around her pale blue irises.

Gulping and trying to stabilize the flames that wanted to erupt out my fingers, I stepped in front of Aspen. We edged cautiously around the trestle table and realized that the kitchen extended beyond where we thought it did.

And there, tied up neatly in a little pen, was a very hairy cow. Complete with dangling udders.

"I guess they get their cream really fresh," I said stupidly.

Aspen had a slightly horrified expression on her face.

"I am going to be severely disappointed if the only cream in this kitchen is...in there." She pointed to the cow. I silently agreed.

"I've never milked a cow." I glanced at my reddened fingers. "And she probably doesn't want blisters on her, uh, lady cow parts."

Aspen snorted. The snort turned into a chuckle, and before long, we were both laughing, trying to hold it in as quietly as we could, lest someone hear us through the open windows.

Minutes later, Aspen wiped tiny little ice crystals from her eyes while I took a deep breath that didn't result in another fit of hilarity.

"Oh, I think I needed that," Aspen said shakily, her cheeks rosy from laughing. I felt lighter, too. Lighter than I'd felt in a long time.

"Me, too."

The cow stared at us with a bored expression on its long face.

"I vote we look for cream elsewhere and use the source as the last resort."

"Agreed," I said quickly. Without meaning to, my hand found the small of her back. She startled, but as I was staring at my hand in frozen shock, she relaxed quickly before I could pull back. Blinking in surprise at my own subconscious audacity, I nudged her towards the larger part of the kitchen, snatching my hand back once my muscles decided to obey.

We looked along the table, finding a crock of pale purplish stuff Aspen assured me was sugar harvested from some fruit or other, hiding behind some lemons. I still didn't see any cream.

"I don't think that cow would like frozen parts any better than blistered ones. I can only go so warm," Aspen lamented.

"Well, don't cows get milked, I don't know, on some sort of schedule?" My knowledge of farm life was nearly non-existent, but I thought I'd read something about that somewhere.

"I have no idea. But if they do, then there has to be milk in here somewhere," Aspen said as she pursed her lips.

"Wait, what's under here?" I found a long piece of muslin draped over the end of one of the counters. Grabbing a metal skewer, I flipped the muslin back.

Low and behold, there were several buckets of milk, cream rising to the top.

"Ah ha!" I whisper-shouted.

"Yes!" Aspen cheered quietly, pumping a fist in the air.

I lugged one of the pails by its metal handle to the granite counter while Aspen gathered a few eggs and the crock of sugar.

"How much trouble do you suppose we'd be in if someone caught us?" I asked as I located a large crockery bowl and handed it to Aspen.

"Well, in our time, it would be several demerits. We'd have a lot of detention and probably clean up duty for a few weeks."

"Wow. Just for sneaking into the kitchen and making ice cream?"

"Some creatures have to have highly regulated food sources and accidental contamination would be very bad."

"Ah. How do you know so much about kitchen punishments?" I lifted an eyebrow at her.

A grin tipped one corner of her mouth. "My best friend's brother Luke. He's never conformed well to rules. Anyway, he and some buddies snuck into the kitchen to make mushroom pizza or something, I don't remember, but I do remember that the Academy came down on them hard once it came to light that they'd accidentally spoiled a week's worth of brandle-berry juice meant to feed some exceedingly particular fae who happened to have the ear of members of the school board. In the end, Luke was probably lucky he wasn't suspended."

I whistled between my teeth.

"All right. So, I know this is what we need for ice cream, but I'm not sure about quantities. Any ideas?" She ran a long finger along the rim of the sugar crock.

"How much ice cream do you want?" I winked.

"Let's start with two eggs. Tip in cream until I say?"

"The bucket is wood. I can touch the handle, but I may set the wood on fire." I sighed.

"You're not radiating as much heat as usual. Try it," Aspen encouraged.

I pressed my lips together, realizing with mixed degrees of shock and satisfaction that while my flames were rushing furiously like white-water rapids, they weren't erratic. There was a pulsing sort of pattern. A tease of control. A delicious heat started curling in my middle, realizing that Aspen had noticed.

"Get ready to ice it if it catches," I said, my fingers twitching, but feeling brave enough to try it.

She stepped close enough our shoulders touched, sending that delicious curl of heat leaping to life.

So slowly I could have been an old man, I grasped the handle, held the bucket aloft, then gingerly touched two fingers to the edge. Using only enough pressure to tip the bucket, I watched in fascination as thick cream plopped into the bowl with a splash of milk over the top. Setting the bucket down, I whipped my fingers off.

Inspecting it and letting out a breath I didn't realize I'd been holding, I couldn't see any marks of charring. Excitement buzzed in my chest. I couldn't remember a time in the past four years that I'd been able to touch any flammable surface without immediate signs of smoke or burning.

"Did you use any ice on that?" I asked her, hoping she hadn't.

"Nope. That was all you. You controlled your flames." Aspen smiled so wide her teeth glinted in the moonlight. Pride shown in her eyes and sent a shiver of pleasure rippling over my shoulders. Before I could help it, my eyes tracked to her lips. I swallowed hard. Mercifully, she'd already turned back to the bowl and hadn't seen my errant gaze.

She added sugar then began to mix with a long-handled wooden spoon.

"I have no idea what this is supposed to look like." She held up the wooden spoon and creamy white glop dripped back into the bowl. She raised a dubious eyebrow then glanced at me. "Any thoughts?"

I shrugged. "I've only ever eaten pre-made ice cream. Never took Magic for Homemakers in school."

She stirred the bowl's contents again. "Me neither. Probably should have. Oh, well. Can you add enough heat to cook the eggs without scrambling them?"

"I can try."

The cow mooed in the background as if in encouragement. Thinking cool thoughts, I gingerly put one finger into the slimy mixture and let it sit. Aspen stirred, and things began to thicken up, but miraculously didn't curdle.

"Perfect. I think," she giggled. The silvery sound of it sent little ripples over my shoulders again. "All right. Ready for the most amazing ice cream you've ever eaten?" She gave me a cheeky grin and my chest tightened in response.

"Let's see it." I stopped myself short of adding *Ice Queen* to the end of my sentence. Not that I meant it in a bad way, it just jumped unbidden into my head.

She held her palm over the bowl and let a fine frigid mist fall over the contents as she continued stirring with her other hand.

It was fascinating. The ice cream froze, and my mouth watered.

"*Bon appetite.*" She handed me a metal spoon and hopped up on the granite counter beside the bowl.

That first spoonful was icy, sweet, and melted as soon as it hit my tongue. But, oh, did it taste good. My eyes slid shut and a small groan of appreciation sounded in my throat.

"Is it edible?"

My eyes opened and I smirked. "Had me taste it first to make sure I didn't keel over?"

"Figured your heat would save you from any impending food poisoning." Her eyes glinted as she teased me.

"It's delicious. Grainy, but really good." I scooped another giant spoonful out of the bowl and watched as Aspen took a bite.

A tiny drop landed on her lower lip. My finger snaked out and gently swiped it off. And then I swallowed hard on a dry mouth as her eyes widened.

"Why did that guy call you Ice Queen?" The words slipped out softly. *Ice Queen* had been rumbling in the back of my brain off and on since before we'd left our time, and now that my heart wanted to get involved, I needed to know what happened.

Her spoon froze halfway to her mouth, and I wanted to kick myself.

She looked at her spoon of ice cream, slowly put it in her mouth, then swallowed.

"The ice cream is good. You're right. It is a little grainy though."

"Yeah." The word scratched out of my throat like it grated against sandpaper.

Aspen sighed and twirled her spoon in the ice cream on her side of the bowl.

"What have you heard?"

"Only rumors. What really happened?"

Her face shuttered as anger, hurt, and betrayal crossed her features. "We'd been flirting for a while." She paused and her throat constricted as she swallowed again. "Things were great. He was nice—always acted like a gentleman and made me feel special. We were the almost-power couple, both of us at the height of popularity, nearly a solid item. He asked me to go to a party with him over on the island. I don't generally like parties. Usually they make me uncomfortable. But Kasin wanted to take me to the party as our first date. The prospect of a first date was exciting. I thought it would be something really special, so I let him talk me into it.

"Things were fine when we got there. We danced and hung out with some friends. I don't know if he drank something or if it was all him, but once it got late and other couples started leaving or pairing off, Kasin took me to one of the outbuildings—there are several old buildings on the island. I guess they use them for storage and stuff mostly. He said he wanted to show me something. That should have been my first clue. But I was enjoying myself and not expecting things to go sour. Anyway, he took me back to one of them, and he started kissing me."

My heart contracted painfully as fire raged through my veins. I wasn't sure I wanted to hear what happened next, but knew I had to know, one way or the other, now that she'd started the story.

Her clear eyes clouded over, and she looked away as she continued, her fingers absently toying with the spoon still stuck in the bowl of ice cream. Tiny ice crystals dropped from her fingertips. I wanted to hold her fingers against mine and melt the physical signs of her distress.

"At first it was okay. I mean, he wasn't a terrible kisser." Her face closed farther, my heart spluttered, and my fists clenched. Angry fires coursed through my veins. "But then he started really getting into it. Like, pushing me against the wall and rubbing up against me. I told him to stop. He tried to put his hand up my shirt and that's when I decided I'd had enough."

She shivered. Ice cream momentarily forgotten, I shoved my clenched fists into my pockets so any flames would be contained within their magicked confines. I hardly dared breathe.

"He didn't stop. He muttered something about me leading him on and that I owed him this while he tried to stick his tongue down my throat, pinned me to the wall, and unzipped his pants."

Her jaw clenched as her pale icy eyes jerked up and bored into mine.

"I didn't owe him a single thing. I said *no*. And when he still didn't stop, I froze the parts of him that shouldn't have been hanging out. Solidly."

A heavy moment of silence hung between us.

Then shocked laughter ruptured from my throat in a burst of relieved amusement.

"You *froze* his *balls?*" I was laughing so hard a tear squeezed out my eye and sizzled on my cheek.

"He stopped," she said with grim satisfaction.

"I bet he did." If I hadn't already detested the guy, I might have been feeling some sympathy pains for him. But if that's what happened, he deserved it. No meant no.

"He made an awful ruckus after that." A smile tipped the corner of her mouth as she scooped another bite of ice cream into her mouth.

"Aspen, you are, without doubt, the most fearsome girl I've ever met." *And it was so hot.*

She gave me a saucy grin and a wink.

"Ice Queen isn't entirely an unearned nickname."

I smiled around my own bite of deliciousness. Relief that the rumors swirling around her hadn't resulted in something more sinister for Aspen made my heart feel lighter. Although things could have gone wrong. Really wrong. I was so glad they hadn't.

She swirled her spoon in her ice cream, mixing in the little ice crystals that had fallen as she shared her story.

I was falling for the Ice Queen. Falling hard.

CHAPTER 29

ASPEN

The liberation and validation I felt at having told Cole my side of the story was amazing. A weight I didn't know I'd been carrying lifted as I glanced at him. The look he was giving me shot tingles into my middle. Amber flecks floated in his dark irises again.

Something unspoken passed between us and his eyes flashed to my lips. My heart picked up and frost thought about forming on the pads of my fingers. Quickly I took another bite of ice cream, though I wasn't sure why I did. I wanted Cole to kiss me.

Didn't I?

He sighed. A heavy noise tinged with despair.

"Cole?"

"What did that red-haired girl say about me?" He stared into his side of the bowl as he said it.

Oh.

I cleared my throat and reminded myself that the rumors about me were unfounded. The ones about Cole probably were, too. Besides, I trusted Cole.

"She said you...you burned your family. That they all died. And that you were forced to go to Magik Prep because no one else would take you."

His eyebrows hiked up his forehead.

"Well. She certainly has a vivid imagination. My parents are both alive and well. Though dad has taught me all he can about how to control my flames. I think you know that he's a fire-drake. Mom is a phoenix. My phoenix blood makes me burn hotter and more intensely than a regular fire-drake does. And then there's my complete lack of ability to control said raging fires," he said bitterly. "So while it's absolutely true that I could burn someone to a crisp," he shuddered and his face clouded over, "my parents seem to be the only ones immune to my intense heat." He savored another bite of ice cream. His side was starting to melt so near his body heat. I sent another fine mist of freeze over it.

"Thanks," he said absently. "There was a time I could control my flames. Without thought, without any effort."

His face contorted like he was remembering something painful. I put my hand over his, braced against the granite. He weakly squeezed my fingers, the pad of his thumb rubbing an arc of heat against mine. I wanted to offer him comfort—but I wasn't sure what to say. I wasn't sure what else was wrong besides his frustration with his lack of control. But he'd been getting better. I'd seen his improvement since we'd been here in this time. His halting words stopped my thoughts and had my eyes riveted to his tortured face.

"Syrai and I had been friends forever. But the summer we turned fourteen, we fell into something more than friendship." His voice cracked and his fingers tightened around mine. "I...I...it was a first kiss for both of us. I didn't know. I didn't know," he whispered as his eyes slid shut in pain. Trepidation lanced through my middle. I wanted to tell him to stop. That he didn't have to tell me what happened. With dread sinking in my gut, I had a good idea where things were headed.

"I kissed her. And my fire surfaced like it never had. It consumed us both. Of course, it didn't hurt me. But Syrai was—is—a nymph. I literally *melted* her." He choked on the words then dragged in an aching breath. "She survived. Barely. She's had twenty-nine surgeries and seven magicked operations. All because of me. Because I'm a monster."

Tears sizzled on his cheeks and my heart broke.

Without thought of whether or not he'd want me to touch him, he needed a hug. He needed to know I wasn't afraid of him.

I scooted off the counter and came around to him. I wrapped my arms around him as he went rigid and made a choked noise deep in his throat.

"I'm so sorry, Cole," I whispered against his chest. "You're *not* a monster. What happened was an accident. A terrible, horrible accident. But that doesn't make you a monster."

"You're the first person besides my parents who has been able to touch me since then without getting hurt. And it terrifies me." His voice was raw. Finally his body lost some of its rigidity and his arms tentatively came up and rested lightly on my back. I squeezed mine tighter around him.

"Your flames can't hurt me, Cole."

With a strangled sob, Cole pulled me hard against him and buried his face in my neck. Hurt for Cole coiled around my chest. I desperately wanted him to know that I wasn't afraid of him. That he didn't need to be afraid of himself. That he wasn't a monster.

We stood that way, wrapped in a layer of heat and freeze with our arms around each other for long minutes. Time seemed to stand still. We said nothing. The ice cream sat forgotten beside us. Finally, Cole broke the silence.

"Are you afraid of me now? Of my fire?" Raw vulnerability still hung in his voice.

"Does it feel like I am?" I laid my cheek on his chest and squeezed my arms around him tighter.

He dragged in a shuddering breath against my hair.

"Cole, you don't have to live in fear of yourself with me. I'm safe. You can't hurt me," I told him again. At least, his flames couldn't. I wasn't so sure he couldn't hurt me otherwise. I was afraid I was becoming invested. I was probably setting myself up for a broken heart. But at that moment, I didn't care.

"Thanks, Aspen."

I refroze the ice cream. We ate the whole bowl. I refused to admit it, but I ate so much I gave myself a slight belly ache. We searched the tower again but found nothing. By the time we'd completed our search, it wasn't long before dawn.

"I think we should call it early and get maybe an hour more sleep before we head out to the river."

"Probably a good idea." I sighed. I was emotionally wrung out after sharing what happened with Kasin, and then hearing what Cole had lived with the past few years. Even my toenails were tired.

We were asleep when Jack and Anna Beth got up, but we roused ourselves enough to eat breakfast with them and then snoozed another few hours. It was roughly noon when we woke, and I could tell I hadn't had enough sleep. My eyelids felt like there was sand trapped underneath them.

Cole groaned.

"I don't know if it's the floor or time travel in general."

A smile tugged at my lips. "Probably both. Let's get a snack and get out to the river. We're going to have to figure out a way to sneak out and back in. Any great ideas?"

"We've gone tumbling nearly a thousand years back in time. Why couldn't we have managed an invisibility cloak, too?"

I was used to Cole's biting sarcasm, but this was different. Some of the darkness that surrounded him was gone.

"Cole, did you just attempt to make a joke?"

"Don't tell anyone. You have no idea how hard it is to maintain the bad boy image so people stay away."

"Do you want me to stay away?" I tried to use a teasing tone, but the words came out softer, and sounding more serious, than I meant them to.

"No, Aspen. I don't."

Heat flooded my pale cheeks before I could stop it and a lazy smile tipped the corner of Cole's mouth, his expression open.

"We'd better go. We're wasting daylight." I struggled with my blanket and then rushed through the door to Anna Beth's room to put myself together.

Fortunately, the school grounds were practically deserted. It must have been a block where everyone was in class, since no one wandered the grounds. Maybe everyone was too scared of Lord Broderick's threats. Briefly I wondered if *we* should be more concerned about them. In our time there were several gates around the property set into the massive walls so people could come and go freely. I doubted that was the case now, since there were dangers, and I knew for a fact, that a war was looming. The thought sent a shiver working over my shoulders.

"There." Cole pointed to a tiny door tucked into the corner of a wall. "If it's locked, I can super heat it so that the lock will spring."

"Look at you, great mastermind of breaking and entering."

"Just exiting," he retorted with a snarky grin.

It didn't take long for Cole to get us through the gate. We crept through the shadows of the wall until we were as far out of sight of the tower as we could get, then quickly made our way down to the river.

"We're going to have trouble getting back in the school grounds if they post a sentry towards evening. They *should* have one posted," Cole commented.

"Surely Jack would have mentioned it if they had decided to. Although I agree, you'd think they would on purpose with Lord Broderick's threats coming in. Unless they don't realize how seriously they should be taking them." I bit my lip. Maybe we should speak to

Jack and impress upon him the importance of taking those threats seriously.

We kept going, both keeping our own thoughts. It was cool and a stiff breeze kept flipping my hair across my face. Grumbling to myself, I found a smallish stick. I knocked the rest of the loose bark off to make it smoother, then twisted my hair into a knot and jammed the stick through it.

"I haven't been to the Chasm or island in our time. What's different?" Cole asked after a few minutes.

"Well," I gazed around. Squinting, I looked at the large hill, not quite a mountain, but certainly a sizable land mass that jutted up from the earth. The river disappeared around the base of it. Scanning to the other side of the hill, I could barely detect a glimmer. "Does it look like the river goes around this hill on three-ish sides to you?" I pointed to the other side where the light glinted off what looked like a silvery snake.

"Yeah. Are you thinking that maybe this hill is what actually became—becomes—the island?"

I tapped my lip. "I mean, there's no glacier. So whatever part of the story has passed into legend was passed on incorrectly. Or we have the wrong war, though I find that unlikely. Maybe a different battle in the same war? But the river still runs through the base of the Chasm in our time, just on all four sides. The river actually splits and circles both sides, making the island."

"Why don't we make our way around to the backside of the hill and check it out. We'll keep our eyes open for strands of magic while we're looking."

"Works for me." I picked my way carefully over the rocks as they dotted over the ground. There were quite a few trees down this close to the riverbank, and the undergrowth wasn't too overgrown. The river made a pleasant rippling noise as it tripped over its path.

"So, tell me something frost fairies do besides freeze unsuspecting body parts?"

I snorted and glanced at Cole. One side of his mouth tipped up as his eyes narrowed in a teasing manner.

I shrugged, still smiling, reveling in the way that sharing the pain of Kasin's betrayal with Cole had lessened it considerably. "I don't know. We freeze things. We make mist, snow, sleet, hail, ice." I shrugged again. "I've heard stories that at the beginning of things, it was the job of the frost fairies to herald in the autumn and winter months. I've also heard stories that my ancestors were two inches tall with wings. I've never seen any family portraits to that end though. No one I know of in my ancestry has been able to fly. No hidden wings."

Cole smiled. "Somehow I'm having trouble picturing you the size of my finger...although flapping around and zapping things with a flurry of ice cryst als..."

"Haha." I raised an eyebrow at him. A few errant embers floated in his dark irises. "What about you—half fire-drake and half phoenix? If you don't mind me asking. You don't have to tell me if you don't want to," I added quickly, not wanting to make him uncomfortable, though I was curious.

His eyebrows rose slightly. "I think we're past that point." He gave me a rueful look tempered with a hint of embarrassment.

A smile toyed at my lips as my belly fluttered.

"What about me?" he repeated. He sighed. "Being a fire-drake would be pretty awesome by itself, I think."

He was quiet for a minute.

"Because...you're a shape shifter?"

"That's a big part of it. When in drake form, I can fly. I *do* have wings. I can soar across the sky. There's a lot of freedom in that. Being a fire-drake means I can breathe flames, and as you know, fire can't hurt me. But there's a lot of danger since I'm part phoenix, too. Like my mother, I have phoenix fire I can shoot out of my eyes. But it somehow merged with my drake flames, and when I shift, my whole body is enflamed. Like, my wings and my tail are constantly on fire like a phoenix when it lights up and sheds its feathers. I'm unstable. Human or fire-drake, I'm a literal powder keg. That's why I'm at Magik Prep. They're kind of my last resort in helping me understand and learn how to control my flames."

"You're grounded."

"Pretty much."

"I'm sorry."

Cole shrugged, shoving his hands in his pockets. "It is what it is."

"If you were, per say, in the middle of a river, you could shift safely," I offered, glancing over at the waves bumping along the surface of the water.

"Yeah, probably. But I think you may be underestimating my size, too."

I arched an eyebrow.

"I'm big. Really big."

"Is that so?" I snorted.

"Mm-hmm." Cole looked at me, teasing light in his eyes.

Color rose in my cheeks, but fortunately, I was spared from focusing on it by a little zing of orange.

"Look!" I took off after the tree where I saw the little squiggle.

"That's a strand of orange magic stuck up there, isn't it?"

"Yes. Jack was right. There *is some* magic out here." Excitement pinged through my middle as we raced for the tree.

It was up too high for either of us to reach.

"Give me a boost, I'll see if I can climb up and get it."

"You know I'd volunteer to do that if I wasn't worried about burning down the tree and the magic," Cole said sourly.

"And you'd get another not-a-jerk-point." I winked and braced my hands on his fire-warm shoulders.

CHAPTER 30

COLE

Breathe, I reminded myself. Fire sped through my veins as Aspen put her hands on my shoulders and I wove my fingers together. The problem was that I was a guy. And Aspen had a very curvy part of her very girly self practically shoved in my face as she stepped on my hands and took a light experimental bounce. I clinched my eyes shut, swallowed hard, and boosted her upwards. It didn't matter. Her boob brushed my head, and I could tell her hips were right at eye-level.

"Cole? Can you go a little higher? I've got a branch, but this stupid skirt is making things more difficult than they should be."

I may have groaned. She was in a skirt. I could not look. But I needed to see the branch she was aiming for so I could lift her.

"Am I that heavy?" She sounded slightly horrified. I must have groaned out loud.

"No, just trying not to burn you to cinders," the excuse slipped out.

"Oh, sorry. I can ice myself more."

I could feel the cold through her shoe. It did nothing to calm the inferno raging inside me. I glanced up, wildly hoping I didn't get an eyeful of something I'd never want to unsee. And caught a full frame of the underside of her chest.

Angling my head around, I could see the branch she was trying to reach. It wasn't like I was having trouble lifting her, just keeping my focus. I raised her higher towards the branch and she caught it easily.

"Got it!"

Her foot left my hand, and then she was up the tree like a winged harpy.

"Yes! Ooh, it's a long piece. It looks pretty well-formed, too. Here. If I bend, I think I can hand it to you. I need both hands to get back down."

She bent over and I was able to reach the dangling end of the magic, but the white top she wore dipped, and I had a clear shot down her shirt. I was going to combust.

"Okay. Got it. I'm good," I croaked. I really hoped I didn't have flames shooting out my ears. Aspen started her descent with a crackle and swish of leaves and bark.

"Catch me!"

I had two seconds before Aspen came floating down from the lowest branch. My hands caught her around the waist, drawing her close so she was flush against me. My heart pounded and flames roared through my head.

I clenched the orange magic hard enough to pulverize it—it was a miracle it wasn't charring—as my eyes landed on her lips, pink and slightly parted. Cool spread over my chest where her hands touched me. Tearing my eyes from her lips, I sought her eyes.

They were big and blue. I ripped myself away from her as the perfect image of Aspen's face merged with my memory overlay of Syrai's melted one after my lips had touched her.

I shuddered, unable to stop myself.

Aspen's face softened. "Come on. There may be more magic up ahead."

Without another word, she took the magic strand in one hand and mine in her other, tugging me forward. After a few steps, my feet stopped stumbling and remembered how to walk on their own. I didn't let go of Aspen's hand.

"Cole!" Aspen jerked to a halt some minutes later.

"What?" I scanned our surroundings but saw nothing.

She shoved the bottom of my black shirtsleeve up a fraction. There, caught on the very rim of my cuff, were a few tiny flecks of magenta dust.

"Where did it come from?" My words sounded breathless.

Aspen, still holding my hand and my sleeve, looked me up and down, searching for more magic, but sending skitters of sparks shooting down my limbs instead.

"Turn around."

I did, and I could feel her eyeballs scrutinizing me.

"I don't see any more. Do I have any on me?"

Was she asking me to check her out?

I held in my smirk, knowing how important this actually was, and checked her over, secretly enjoying every second.

"I don't see any magenta dust." While I enjoyed an excuse to really look at her, it was disappointing to find nothing

Aspen sighed in frustration. "It's here. It's obviously here. We've found it twice now—at least dust, or remnants of what we need. But where is it? Where's the source—the strands that we need to get home?" She paced the grass in agitation, hands on her hips.

"So, we keep looking." I surprised myself by reaching for her. Her cool fingers willingly slid into my hot palm. "Come on. Let's keep going around the backside of the mountain. We've got several hours of daylight still. I'd like to make a full lap. We can check back at this spot again on the way back if you want."

"All right." Her chin quivered and she turned away from me.

"Hey." I tugged her hand. "We're going to be okay. Whether it's in this time or back in our own, I promise, we're going to be okay." Pressure built in my chest as the responsibility of the words I'd just uttered fell on me. I meant it. My fires raced through me, conforming to the desire to fulfill my promise. I'd make sure Aspen was okay. Resolve filtered into my flames, building them, though they stayed contained.

She sniffed and nodded. "Sorry. Okay. Let's go."

I squeezed her hand, giving her a minute. She brushed a few errant crystals away with the back of her finger. Glancing up at me and giving me a watery smile, she took a step, and we kept moving along the river's edge.

We made our way in comfortable silence, both scanning like hawks for anything magical. Once we were truly at the backside of the mountain, the Academy completely hidden from view, we came up to a pile of scrubby brush that was about chest high a short distance from the river bank.

"This stuff is prickly." Aspen frowned at an offending stick.

I worried the inside of my lip. "And it looks pretty dry." Glancing down at my hands, they weren't as red as they usually were. I flexed my fingers. No flames threatened to erupt.

"It looks like it parallels the river for a while. I don't suppose there's any point in going straight through it. We can make our way over the riverbank until the scrub gets more manageable."

"Good idea." Relief coursed through me as I realized I wouldn't have to worry long about setting the brush alight.

We trudged through the rocky sand a few more minutes. The sun glinted sharply up ahead.

I sucked in a breath. "Aspen, wait." The words hissed between my teeth.

She froze. The breeze changed direction and words floated softly to us, near enough to hear snatches of voices, but not close enough to hear words.

Aspen's eyes widened as we looked at each other. She held up one finger then flicked her wrist.

A cold breeze, stronger than the last, came whistling down the side of the mountain, bringing the words with it clearly.

"He said they'd be ready. The walls have several weaknesses that we can exploit. And underneath..." A male voice said.

"This intel better be solid. You know His Highness won't stand for aught," another answered.

"Do you doubt my word?" The first voice grew agitated.

Aspen flicked her wrist and brought another gust of conversation to us. I didn't dare breath.

"Your word, I trust. But a turncoat's? That is always questionable. Where is Jorgin?"

"He's right here."

We whirled around, only to meet the point of a drawn sword held by a tall man clad in medieval plate armor with chain mail covering his head.

"Eaves dropping, were we?" His deep voice seemed to echo in the valley.

Adrenaline pounded in my brain and flames coursed through my arms so hard that they shook. One thought shot through my whole body.

Protect Aspen.

CHAPTER 31

ASPEN

Snow fell from my fingers and my skirt whooshed out around me as we spun towards the voice. I'd been so intent on gathering the words from the others that I hadn't heard this man approach. My mouth was dry, my palms caked in a sheen of ice.

We were in so much trouble.

Before I could process anything else, Cole tore his hand from mine and shoved me away. I tripped and went down hard on the ground.

Ripping flesh and a thud that shook the ground bashed my senses as a deep throated roar rattled my bones.

Then heat. So much heat.

I threw my hands over my head and encased myself in a bubble of ice before I dared look up.

The world was on fire.

All I could see from my crouched position on the ground were massive back legs and the fiery points of wings that ended in live flames. And the spots that blurred my vision caused by my pulse hammering through every inch of me.

Cole. Where was Cole?

Another roar blasted and my hands clapped over my ears. Terror clawed at my throat and my hair froze stiff where my hands touched my temples

Then it hit me.

Cole *was* the fire!

I scrambled to my feet, disintegrating the bubble of ice I'd made, and dashed to the side of one of Cole's legs, as thick as a tree trunk.

He hadn't been kidding when he said he was big.

The man, Jorgin, was scrambling away on all fours like a crab, trying to clutch his heavily burned arm to his chest, his face blistered and sweating.

Screeching twisted through the treetops, and I whipped around in time to see three black Pegasus horses shooting across the sky. Their massive hooves skimmed the trees as majestic wings pounded the air.

As I turned back to the injured man in front of us, another black Pegasus alighted in front of him, prancing and agitated, panicked in Cole's presence. The full whites of the horse's eyes showed around the dark irises. Froth foamed at its mouth.

Jorgin dug his less burned hand into the black mane and hauled himself up. The pair sped off into the air like the blast of a magicked cannon.

Thunder rumbled in Cole's chest, and I put a hand against his leg.

Glancing fully up to his face for the first time, I had to tip my head way back. Then I had to squint.

My breath caught in my lungs. His face was wreathed in flames, eyes like twin suns blazing from the middle of a burst of lightning. He had two horns, a frill ending in flames behind his head, and a row of fire streaked down his back to a long, whip-like tail, thrashing and alight with flames. Sizzles and great billows of steam rose where his tail flipped into the river.

His wings blocked out the sun, but the shadows wavered and flickered as the living fire inside him danced in the natural light.

I let myself start to thaw as my heart rate slowly descended back into a normal pattern.

Cole was still looking around, his head craning on his long neck.

Are you all right?

Startling at the voice echoing inside my head, I squinted up again. I raised a hand against the brightness that was Cole's face. The voice had belonged to Cole, but it was deeper, dragonish.

"I'm fine. Are...are you okay?"

Cole nodded then angled his head to the sky. His massive chest expanded as his eyes slid shut. Coals crackled along the ridged scales across his abdomen. With a piercing scream, he let loose a mighty column of fire straight into the sky. Clouds hissed into oblivion as his flames seared past them.

Once his fire was spent, he turned away from me.

Hands still covering my ears, mouth gaping, and eyes bigger than a polly goggle's, I watched as Cole began to shrink back into himself, his flames retracting until he was once again a boy. His shirt was burned in places showing his pale skin underneath as smoke rose from his shoulders and hair.

"Oooh," he groaned tiredly and slumped to his knees, head bowed.

"Cole!" I rushed to him, plopping unceremoniously to the sooty ground beside him. "Are you hurt?" My hands fluttered near him, unsure if I should touch him or not. My heart was in my throat, and a few stray ice crystals may have squeezed out the corners of my eyes.

"I'm fine," he rasped. "Are you sure you're not hurt? I didn't burn you? You...you're totally fine?"

I spread my arms. "Not even singed." I let my hands fall back to my sides, then glanced around us. The surrounding vegetation couldn't say the same. Quickly sending a shower of ice over a few still-flaming spots, I put out the rest of the fires still burning around us. Turning back to Cole, I tentatively reached out a hand to rest on his arm.

He bowed his head again but did not pull away from my touch. I blinked and inhaled a lungful of charred air. Glancing down, I realized we were in the middle of a deeply scorched patch, one little bubble of green remaining to the right where I'd encased myself in ice.

"We need to get back to the Academy. Half the world will have seen that jet of fire I just let loose." He groaned and ran his hands through his smoky hair. "That felt so good. I haven't purged like that in weeks."

"Maybe you should more often?"

"Probably."

"Cole, your hair has changed again."

"Yeah? Still look kinda hot?"

His black eyes held that cheeky snark again and I felt myself blushing. Swallowing, I tried to regulate, though I'm not sure I managed well after all the excitement.

"It's still kinda hot," I confirmed. "Literally and figuratively," I teased. "More a coppery-bronze color now. Still gold at the tips and black at the roots."

"Good to know. Come on." He grabbed my hand and we struggled to our feet then picked our way through the blackened ground in order to be well away from the river before anyone from the Academy could get out here to investigate too closely.

"I think the war is on the figurative and literal horizon," Cole said as we made our way back into the lush grasses.

"I know. We've got to find that magic. And warn Jack."

CHAPTER 32

COLE

I was cold. Not numb like I'd shut off my emotions the way I'd spent most of the last four years. Like, literally cold. I marveled, trying to wrap my head around what could have caused a sudden surge of cool as we walked quickly back along the riverbank towards the school. My fire was still there. It raged happily along every vein in my body. But I still felt cool. I'd never felt like this after a purge, although admittedly, I hadn't purged flames like that in...well, I'd never shot flames with that kind of triumphant frustration before.

This weird sense of satisfaction hung around my shoulders. I'd had a purpose for my flames. They'd protected Aspen. I'd succeeded in keeping her safe. I'd acted on my promise. That was the only thought I'd had as my skin split and fire leaked out every pore until my scales covered them up.

"Aspen, is my skin...less hot than normal?"

I couldn't tell. I was some strange juxtaposition of hot and cold. The heat inside me was intense, but the outside of me—almost like an outer shell—felt shockingly devoid of flames.

"Sorry, I wasn't really paying attention. Let me go back to my normal temperature."

She let go of my hand and her face went one shade pinker.

We were still walking; neither of us wanted to explain who we were, what we were doing, and that I'd just torched some would-be invader should we run into Academy people on the way to check out the smoke I'd raised. She slipped her hand back into mine.

Her mouth tugged down at the sides, and she brought us both to a full stop. She touched my arm. Touched my skin through one of the burned patches over my chest. Touched my forehead. I tried to keep my breathing steady but wasn't entirely successful. My temperature started to rise as her hands fluttered over me.

"Cole. You're *not* hot. You're never not hot. What's going on?"

I took her hand and started walking again.

"Honestly, I don't know. Maybe purging the flames?"

"Are they still there?"

"Oh yeah, they're there. I could still combust at any second." Probably sooner rather than later if we stopped to further explore the heat content of more of my skin.

"Has it ever happened before?"

"Not since," I swallowed, "not since Syrai." My voice came out all husky as I said her name. Guilt and fear still gnawed at me every time I pictured her face. I cleared my throat. "I mean, I still purge the fires every so often, but it's never made me cold like this." I stopped. "Not since I lost control of my fire."

"Is this what control feels like?" she asked softly as she squeezed my fingers. Her other hand skimmed my forearm, raising gooseflesh beneath my tattered shirt sleeve and setting a sweet heat thrumming through me.

I hardly dared to think the words. Was it possible? Could some fluke have caused me some measure of control again? Could it be Alger-Aodh's blessing? Was it something about this time? Was it Aspen?

"I can't remember," I whispered.

We were quiet as we neared where we'd veered off into the high brush.

"It's there, behind the back of the mountain!" a voice called. Much closer than was comfortable.

Aspen's eyes met mine, wide and surprised. We ducked down into the river weeds and scrunched ourselves behind the trunk of the widest tree. Flames coursed warmer under my skin but didn't reach flammable levels on the outside.

I hoped they didn't have any creatures with particularly good smell, or that there was still enough general smokiness in the air that they couldn't sniff us out hiding in the tangle of grasses.

"Wait for me!" a female called.

"Come on. Move your paws!" came the gruff reply.

"I thought the fire-drake was keeping to himself these days. Doesn't he schedule his great bursts of flame?" someone puffed.

"You know he does as he pleases. He's one of the founders. You think they'd go against him if he wanted to take an unsanctioned trip off Academy grounds?" The gruff voice grew more impatient.

Slowly the voices faded, and oxygen entered my lungs.

"That was close," Aspen whispered near my ear.

"They made it out here faster than I anticipated. We need to move." Urgency kicked adrenaline through me, shooting it to my extremities.

"What if they have patrols running the top of the Academy walls?" Aspen worried her lip as I slowly rose up and glanced around. Seeing no one else, I motioned for her, and we started moving again.

"Then you'll get to show me how big a frigid mist you can make."

The walls rose like stark yellow cliffs from the grassy, rock-strewn plain surrounding the Academy. Sure enough, there were clusters of bodies peppering the tops of the walls so far as we could see from our vantage behind the last few trees that separated us from the wide-open space before the safety of the shadows from the Academy.

"This would be a great time to have a magicked mobile and call a friend to make a diversion while we slipped in the side gate." I didn't miss the heavy note of sarcasm in Aspen's voice.

"Assuming you had friends to call," I quipped. I wouldn't have had anyone to call back in our time even if we'd been there.

"Touché. I guess we're both kind of on the outs there. But now you have me. I'd create a diversion for you." She winked at me, and my lips tugged up in response.

"Remind me to get your number if we ever make it back to our time."

"When." I didn't miss the desperation in her voice.

"When," I amended.

"I suppose it's more logical for a heavy mist to roll in with the evening, rather than in late afternoon." Aspen sighed.

"You're probably right. It would be less conspicuous, plus there'd be more shadows, if we wait another hour or so. I'm guessing it's about an hour and a halfish until sunset?"

"It's hard to tell. I'm used to having a watch on all the time. The one I was wearing didn't survive the trip back here."

We watched the creatures milling on the walls. There was a nervous energy about them. Some huddled together. Some clung to tall spears. Some fidgeted, pacing back and forth. But what was clear was that the surrounding area was being watched like never before.

My spurt of flames had wrecked all chance of us getting back into the Academy unseen, but maybe it had been enough to prompt sentry duty. Unfortunately, we were on the outside of the wall when it happened. My temperature began to rise again and the protective layer of cold I'd felt during our walk back began to fade.

"Cole, your skin is steaming through your shirt." She brushed the hair off my forehead. "Your thumbprint isn't glowing though."

I glanced down at my shirt. This could be a problem.

"Crap. My clothes. Obviously, I burned through some of the magic woven in them." I ran a hand through my hair. "Because of the magic they're supposed to shift with me. But they also keep my heat in. Without them covering my skin, there's nothing between my fire and the rest of the world." Panic nudged my heat up another notch and one hole—the hole Aspen had touched my skin through earlier—began smoking.

Quickly, Aspen put her hand over the spot, and the relief of her icy palm pressed against my chest stilled some of the panic.

"I have an idea." Her face took on a determined expression.

She dug in the pocket of her skirt and pulled out the now slightly rumpled piece of orange magic.

"It's not a perfect solution, but I did take Magic for Everyday Living my freshman year. I should be able to do basic clothes repairs. It probably won't be super pretty to look at, but I think I can patch your shirt."

"Anything is better than burning away the one protective layer I've got." Relief was sweet and scorched through me, leaving a tingling trail in its wake.

She cleared her throat as her cheeks flashed pink before fading back to their normal paleness. "I will need your shirt though."

"Oh." I wasn't self-conscious enough to care if she saw me with my shirt off—the thought actually sent a fresh wave of heat up my spine—but I was concerned about being too hot without the last shreds of my shirt over my skin. "Is there any way you can keep me from incinerating our immediate surroundings?"

CHAPTER 33

ASPEN

My stomach did a little flip flop as Cole looked over at me with vulnerable, hopeful eyes. The thought of sitting next to him, touching some part of him while I held his shirt in my hands, attempting to fix it, and keeping the cool going through both of us, sent little skitters of something wildly exciting over my skin and prickled up the hairs on my arms. I cleared my throat and attempted to speak without squeaking.

"Probably?" I still squeaked.

In the end, Cole sat, bare chested, chiseled like a marble demi-god, arms propped on one raised knee while his other leg was extended, boot off, his foot pressed against mine. My shoe sat neatly in the grass beside his. I'd never made ice flow into someone using my toes before, but for the moment, it was working.

I felt the weight of his eyes on me as I examined the different sized holes burned through his shirt. Fingering the orange magic, I let my own magic seep into it, binding little bits of myself and my ice into the orange strand. The magic nearly doubled in size and turned a little muddied in color but was strong and supple. Exactly what I needed.

Now, if I could remember the correct sequences of bends and twists to make it stick and meld with the fabric properly.

Catching my lip between my teeth, I let my fingers smooth over the soft cotton knit of the long-sleeved waffle print. A faint scent of smoke, cinnamon, and something distinctly Cole that reeked of *male* sent my head spinning.

"Aspen, you okay?" Cole's toes nudged mine, triggering another shot of iciness from my foot into his. "Your eyes are all 'faun in the spotlight.'"

"Yeah. Making sure I remember the pattern right." It had nothing to do with shirtless Cole sitting beside me. Nothing at all. Pulling my mind back to the task at hand, I traced the opening of one of the holes with my finger.

You can do this, I told myself. With another quick inhale, I set my fingers to work. I hadn't ever done a repair this intricate or covering this much of any one garment.

It took longer than I expected, trying to stretch the strand over each and every singed spot and gaping hole in the cloth. Fortunately, it did play nicely with the magic remains still threaded heavily throughout the shirt.

"There." I held up the top in triumph and tried not to wince at the end result. While I had successfully patched every hole, the shirt was now black with some frayed neon bits of magic melding into brown or orange frizzy-looking bits. It wasn't pretty. "Well, I did tell you it probably wouldn't be attractive."

"If it keeps my flames contained, it will be perfect. Thank you." The gravity in his tone told me how much he appreciated my efforts and my cheeks flushed for the umpteenth time that day before I could stop them.

"You're pretty when you blush."

My eyes flew to his. A crooked grin sat on his lips and amber flecks swirled slowly around his black irises. His toes nudged mine again.

"Really. Thank you. This..." He shrugged. "This is really important to me."

I smiled. My toes nudged his back. "You get another not-a-jerk point."

He grinned then glanced at the sky, awash in lively colors and fading into darkness at the edges. "Yeah, well, it's nice to drop the jerk act." His grin was boyish. "Think it's dark enough for some mist to roll in?" he asked, switching gears.

"Probably." My fingers twisted into the material still in my hands. "Oh, here's your shirt." I quickly passed it over to him, trying not to ogle his abs as they contracted when he reached an arm out to grab his clothes.

I was not entirely successful. Cole caught me. He smirked. I wasn't sure if I wanted to kiss him or freeze him. Instead, I slipped my shoe back on and waited for Cole to finish.

"Oh wow. What did you do to this? It's like an ice pack."

"Is it okay?" Anxiety crept into my voice.

"It's awesome!" He did a few experimental movements with his shoulders. "This is the best clothes have ever felt. Will it stay this way?"

"Probably at least to an extent. I put a little frost magic into the orange strip to make it longer. I needed more to cover all the holes in your shirt."

"You're a genius." He laced his boot as I warmed at his praise.

He stood and reached down to help me up. I twined our fingers and looked at the Academy walls. The sun was going down in its mighty brilliance and shadows were starting to creep in at the edges of the plain.

"I hope this works."

"Me, too." He squeezed my fingers then let them go so I could use both my hands.

"You'll want to stay close. If I make a frosty mist thick enough to hide us, it's going to be easy for us to lose each other. Take a good long look at where we're going. There's not going to be much visibility. It's your job to steer us to the Academy. I'm going to be occupied keeping mist rolling over the grassy areas, and not only around us so we don't accidentally target ourselves. Got it?" I could hear the nerves in my own voice.

"Got it," Cole said softly. He trailed a finger down the side of my cheek and swallowed. Quickly, he turned to memorize the path we'd take to the school. "Ready." He dipped his head to me, coppery-golden locks brushing over his forehead, and gently grasped my elbow. "Okay if I hold onto you here?"

I nodded. "Here we go."

Spreading my palms out facing the sky, I let the freeze spill out of me like a bursting dam. Mist, cold and thick, bloomed from my hands and curled to the ground like heavy smoke, twisting away from us in great fluffs of miniscule frozen droplets. It only took a few moments for a wide swath of icy haze to swirl along the ground. With a flick of my wrist and two fingers, a chill puff of wind caught the film and began to spread it further and further. Focusing on making the mist and the wind go where I wanted, we cautiously stepped forward from the cover of the trees.

"Lead me," I whispered. Cole's hand tightened on my arm. My heart pumped with excitement and dread. Anna Beth's skirt snagged on something hiding in the white-washed ground. I hoped I didn't tear it.

Heart in my throat and fine white mist covering everything in our path, above, below, and around us, we stumbled our way across the lea.

Cole bit back a curse as his boot connected with a stone.

"All right?" I whispered. I had no idea how close we were to the walls.

"Fine."

When muted, distorted voices began to filter in through the fog, I knew we were close. Cole heard them, too, and nudged us slightly to the left of the way we'd been heading. The voices grew stronger.

"Ghosts roam on nights like this."

"They're just tales. Naught real of 'em."

"What was that? A Banshee? Did anyone else hear that wailing?"

"Willis, you're imagining things."

"Banshees—they bring bad blood. And death. They always bring death."

Squinting, I saw Cole's fingers graze the side of the stone walls. I let myself have one breath of near-relief. We were almost there. We only needed to find and get through the side gate, then make it back to Jack's.

The voices continued to trickle in as we painstakingly followed the curve of the wall to where we thought the side door was located.

A loud snap to our right sent a fresh plume of mist wafting out of my palms as Cole's hands found my waist, pushing me closer to the building and slightly behind him. I sent an extra poof of mist around us as his heat ratcheted up, burning off some of my mist into steam, creating a little pocket of warmth around us.

"We're back!" called from what sounded like mere feet to our right, blanketed in my eerie fog.

"Open the gate and bring a torch. This fog is so thick I can barely see my hands in front of my face!"

"Orley, that you? Everyone with you—the whole party?" someone called down from the wall.

"We're all here!"

"Miraculously," someone else muttered.

My heart pounded. We could use this as our opportunity to sneak in with the group that was apparently only now returning from the river. Cole's hands squeezed around my waist and steered me towards the voices.

A creak sounded and a faint orange glow appeared in front of us.

"Here now. Torch is right here. Come to my voice!"

"Anyone track down that infernal fire-drake? He could make himself useful and burn off all this mist, you know," the grouser said. There were a few grumbles in response.

We caught the tail end of the party and the door shut snugly behind us, the drop bar *thunking* into place.

"Blast it all, you've brought the mist in with you. It's freezing!"

"Unnatural."

"Sent by our enemies, no doubt."

"You know there's every possibility this is Lord Broderick's fault. He's made his threats. What if this is the time he carries through on them? What if he's hired a sorcerer to enchant us all?"

Even the normally cool blood in my veins iced at the mention of the enemy. I had no doubt that the ruler of Dhoria was responsible for the men on the Pegasi today. Men who would have tried to do who knows what to us if Cole hadn't stepped in first.

Thinking about the way Cole rushed between me and danger brought a wave of heat that nearly sputtered the tiny ice crystals leaving my palms. Shaking my head, I renewed my focus and plumed another curl of frozen vapor into the air.

Cole slid his hand back to my elbow. We could try to sneak through the shadows now.

A shriek pierced the star-studded sky and a startled flurry of snowflakes mixed with the mist falling from my hands. Cole nearly crushed me as he whipped his arm around me and hurried us towards Jack's cottage.

"That's a fire-drake," he breathed as we rushed.

Flames lit the night sky. My mouth dropped open as great golden wings beat steadily above the walls, soaring into the darkness, a stream of fire burning away my freeze like a bonfire melts a frost.

"Alger-Aodh." The murmured words were whisked away from my mouth as Jack's cottage came into view. Cole didn't wait for us to be discovered but shuffled us both straight for the thatched house.

Jamming open the door, he shoved me inside and all but slammed the door behind us.

His chest heaved and he ran both hands through his tri-toned hair. A spurt of frizzed magic looked like a sprout of orange hair dangling from his armpit.

"Where have you been?" Anna Beth whisper-shrieked at us from the kitchen. I could see strands of white-blonde hair falling from her usually perfectly-styled coif. Her cheeks were flushed, and her shoulders were tense.

"Where's Jack?" Cole's voice was tired and old. His body sagged as I glanced at him. I wondered if using so much of his fire today had left him as drained as I was feeling now that the adrenaline wasn't pumping so strongly.

"Trying to find out where all this mist is coming from—whether or not we're under attack!" Anna Beth's voice rose, and her hands clenched and un-clenched, slick with nervous ice.

Guilt thumped me on the back. "Sorry. I caused the mist. We had to find a way to get back into the Academy. With everyone out on the walls, we couldn't think of any way to sneak across the flatlands." I tried to alleviate some of her concern, knowing what we had experienced today would not bring her any comfort when she found out.

"You know, Lord Broderick's threats didn't come until after you got here. What if you're the cause of his new wave of threats?" Her voice was shrill, and terror lurked in her eyes. Though I knew her words were born out of fear, my heart still constricted.

We knew a war was coming. The history we were taught back in our time confirmed it. But what if we *had* somehow triggered something that caused the war itself? My mouth hung open, but no words came out. Anxiety churned in my middle as a heavy sense of dread sat on my shoulders, wrapping around me and squeezing like a Titanoboa.

"That's enough, Anna Beth." Jack had never sounded so stern. My eyes flew to the doorway where he stood wreathed in shadows. He came fully into the room and shut the door with a hard *click*.

"That's enough," he repeated, gentler. "Lord Broderick has opposed the Academy since its founding. Our freedom here, and the freedom the Academy represents, is a threat to him and his tight-fisted rule. He's made periodic threats for three decades. What is happening now is not Cole and Aspen's fault."

Anna Beth hung her head as a few snowflakes drifted to the floor around her. Though she said nothing, her jaw was clenched tight, her fingers fisting against her long skirt.

Jack turned to us. "You are both unharmed?" He searched quickly over our persons, scanning for obvious injury. Satisfied, he turned to me. "You produced all the mist?"

"I did. Sorry to have caused so much trouble. We couldn't think of another way to get into the Academy without being seen, and you made it adamantly clear that our being here was to remain a secret." I bit the inside of my cheek, wondering now if that choice had been the right one.

"Quite right, quite right." Jack sunk into his overstuffed chair. "And you. You somehow triggered the great column of smoke, Cole?"

"I did, although maybe not the way you imagine." Cole glanced at me, and I nodded. "We were nearly attacked today. I think your Lord Broderick is making his move."

Anna Beth gasped as the clink of ice crystals chimed against the flagstone floor.

Jack's eyes riveted to Cole's face.

"Speak," he demanded.

"There were at least four men that we saw. All dressed in battle gear—plate armor and swords—and on black Pegasi. We were able to catch part of their conversation. One of them talked about weaknesses in the wall and something about underneath the school, I think," Cole explained.

"And they spoke of getting their information from a turncoat. Someone inside the Academy has betrayed you," I added.

Cole nodded before continuing as Jack's only response was his furious twisting of his beard. "One of the men snuck up behind us. I shifted to my fire-drake form, and they all scattered. I should have thought better of it, but at the time after all the adrenaline, a purge was getting pretty pressing, so I let my fire belly empty. That's probably part of what you saw. And

I scorched a pretty big patch of earth, which caused some of the smoke."

Jack sat in stunned silence as we all looked on. Anna Beth wrung her hands, a tiny pile of ice growing at her feet.

"So it begins at last." Jack's whispered words hung in the air like daggers ready to fall.

"You think Lord Broderick is making his move." It wasn't a question. I voiced the words I knew were true in my gut.

"I can see no other alternative." Jack blinked, both hands fisted into his beard. "I knew his advances were getting more violent, though I did not truly think he would move his army against the Academy. If he has sent scouts, and what you overheard is true, then I have been grossly mistaken. I wish I had been correct. We are not as prepared as we should be." Jack seemed to age a hundred years there in his chair. Tension coiled inside me, icing my insides in dread. Anna Beth wept softly where she still stood in the kitchen. Terror pinged around my insides like a pixie on steroids. Jack continued twisting his beard, staring straight ahead, then added like an afterthought, "Alger-Aodh wants to see you both in the library tonight. He says its urgent, but to wait and come right before midnight. I think he's seen something. Possibly about the war and the two of you."

CHAPTER 34

COLE

Jack's words stunned me. Alger-Aodh wanted to see us? Finally? My heart sped up and I clenched my fingers into my palms to minimize the risk of sparking. Maybe, in spite of what had happened today, maybe the great fire-drake could still help me—explain what he'd done to me when he blessed me, and let me beg him to help me control my flames. Desperation clawed at my gut. I wanted so badly to be able to be *normal*. Be a part of regular society. Ask Aspen out. Take her out to dinner without fear of setting the restaurant on fire. Part of it was probably the stress and all the crazy that had happened today, plus my body calling for sleep and food. I was exhausted. Mostly in a good way, but my body and my brain were tired. I was short on sleep, high on adrenaline, and low on fuel. Eating needed to be on the priority list.

"Cole, you're shaking," Aspen whispered and stepped closer to me.

"Fuel reserves are about gone." My words chittered as the shaking intensified.

"You need to eat. Now." She cast a worried glance over me then took the initiative and walked into the kitchen.

I nodded, though she'd already turned and couldn't see.

Jack sprang into action. "Right. Food. Let's slice the bread. There's ham still and some fruit." He prattled as his hands became a flurry of action. Anna Beth moved woodenly behind her father and reached for plates.

"Here, let me. Go sit, Anna Beth." Aspen took over, compassion in her voice. Anna Beth walked to her father's chair like one controlled by a spell.

My arms twitched and my fingers spasmed. I needed to eat *soon*. Flames coursed through my digits, wiggling, turning, demanding to be let loose. Tiny cracks began to appear in the flesh of my fingers, molten lava rushing to escape. My head spun as dizziness wrapped me in a cocooning shroud of confusion. "Aspen," I called weakly, knowing I was about to lose my grip on the inferno inside me. Sinking to the floor like I was boneless, I put my palms against the cool stone, desperate to diffuse the heat any way I could.

"Cole!" Aspen said. Suddenly a wave of cold relief flooded up my arms. "Here." Aspen shoved a sandwich in my hand as hers moved to my shoulder, icing me, and bringing my senses into focus. Eyes focused and limbs cooperating, I nodded appreciatively and weakly gripped the sandwich, my fingers burning the bread on contact. First bite swallowed, my jitters started to slow. Shoving more into my mouth, my body regained some semblance of control. To my immense relief, my fires calmed, the rage inside simmering. The flaming pin pricks dancing at the corners of my vision stopped and mental clarity returned.

That had been intense. I'd never emptied myself so completely. I didn't want to do that again.

"You okay now?" Aspen asked, her concerned face still hovering near mine.

"Yeah," I croaked. "Thanks for sending the ice," I said as I ate another bite.

Her eyebrows drew together. "Cole, I didn't. You were cold to the touch. Like your fire was gone. It was terrifying."

"What?" I stopped mid-chew. "How is that possible?"

"I don't know. You're warmer now, but still not normal. Maybe you can ask Alger-Aodh?" Her eyes were hopeful, her hand still on my shoulder. I nodded. Aspen smiled, squeezed my shoulder then went to get her own plate, leaving me to ponder her words. My eyes tracked to Anna Beth who sat like a wooden fence post in her father's chair. Her eyes were blank, her face slack.

"Anna Beth?" I called.

A muscle in her cheek twitched.

"This is your fault," she hissed between her teeth.

Indignant anger boiled under my skin, but I held it in, refusing to let it pour out my mouth. Whether or not Lord Broderick's impending attack was our fault, and I doubted it was, we hadn't tried to come here. We hadn't wanted to come here.

"Anna Beth, we didn't do any of this on purpose. Our being here is an accident," Aspen said, overhearing.

"Daughter. You are over-wrought." Jack spoke kindly, coming to Anna Beth and cupping her cheek. Anna Beth turned away, her shoulders shaking.

Aspen caught my eye and jerked her head towards the door. Nodding, I scooped up the remains of my sandwich, hauled myself to my feet, and followed her to the door.

We slipped out into the darkness. There were still some creatures milling about. A faun near the school building, sentries on the walls, an impossibly tall fae across the courtyard.

Keeping to the shadows, we were able to make it to the doors of the school building without drawing any unnecessary attention. The door protested on its hinges, but with a graze of intentional heat from me, the hinges let us in without further objection.

The halls were deserted.

"Should we go ahead and go to the library?" Aspen whispered.

I shrugged. "I guess. I don't know where else to go at this point. We've probably got a few hours before

Alger-Aodh will come." I stuffed the last of my sandwich into my mouth as Aspen nibbled on hers.

We snuck to the library without a chance meeting with any Brownies or the ogre.

Must, dust, and the ancient smell of parchment met us as we moved into the enormous room.

Aspen yawned, triggering one of my own.

"I'm seriously contemplating a nap," she said, glancing about the dark room.

"Let me warn you that the floor is hard. But I could go for a nap myself."

Eventually we settled together near the granite staircase and finished our sandwiches. Aspen had packed two more in her pocket, which I appreciated. I was still hungry and concerned about my fuel reserves. But once I'd eaten more, I felt full and sleepy. I propped my back up against the stone, leery of falling too deeply asleep in an unprotected area. Aspen rested her head on my shoulder, her shiny hair falling over me like cornsilk.

Moments later, her even breathing told me she was asleep. My eyelids drooped, my heart content for the moment with Aspen next to me. It was strange, to be so content while still aware of the impending danger surrounding the Academy and possibly impacting whether or not we'd ever see our own home again. My eyes closed.

Sometime later I woke with a crick in my neck, which I quickly forgot about as I realized Aspen was still sleeping against me, one of her arms casually thrown across my waist, her head on my chest.

My heart thumped. She trusted me. Completely. In spite of the damage I caused wherever I went.

Syrai's ruined face flashed across my memories, her screams of terror and pain clashing in my ears causing me to wince.

"Cole?" Aspen sat up sleepily, her hand finding my chest right over my drumming heart.

"I'm here." The words were strangled and tight in my throat.

"What's wrong?"

I sighed. How did I tell her I had fallen for her? How could I tell her that after what happened with Syrai? That I wanted her but could never have her? The possibility of hurting her was too great. Even if she was the Ice Queen, I was still afraid the monster inside me might rear its head again and melt her completely. Even if the monster had been strangely subdued of late.

My hand trailed down her hair.

"Do you suppose Alger-Aodh will be dropping by anytime soon?" I asked instead. I didn't want to move, but some distance between us would help me clear my head. My insides were burning up with her pressed against me.

"I have no idea what time it is."

"Me neither. My back needs to pop," I said, needing space before I did something stupid.

"I could stretch, too."

I stood stiffly and reached a hand down to pull her to her feet.

Her hand was cool and delicate in my hot grasp. As she straightened, her chest brushed mine and without knowing how it happened, my hands were suddenly on her waist.

Electricity charged the air between us.

I felt the sparks floating in my eyes and the burning she caused inside me threatened to explode. Different from my usual fire, but with no less potential for destruction. Hers.

Aspen's hand snaked out and cupped my jaw.

Her breath was cool on my face. My knees went weak.

"Aspen." Her name was a plea on my lips.

Hers were pink and parted, inches from mine. My fingers tightened around her waist, sitting directly above the curve of her hips. Blood and fire crashed through me, threatening to burst me wide open.

"Cole, do you want to kiss me?"

"You know I do," the words rasped themselves from my throat. My pulse pounded and her skin was frigid beneath her shirt and my burning hands.

"Your fire won't hurt me. It can't hurt me." Her whisper of cool breath hit my face and my resolve crumbled. Her lips were an inch away from mine. Longing made my flaming limbs tremble. Her chest was pressed against mine and I couldn't tell if the frantic beating was my heart or hers.

Her hand slid up my neck and into the hair at the base of my neck.

I think I groaned.

Quick as lightning, she grazed her lips across mine. I jerked back, terrified wanting searing through me. The taste of her melted on my lips.

Her fingers rested against the pulse pounding in my neck. She bore no blisters. No marks of my heat. She was not Syrai. She was frost. She was snow. She was ice.

She was waiting. Her blue eyes were clear. With a shiver of pleasure, I realized she wanted *me* to kiss *her* as much as I wanted to.

Something broke within me and for the first time in four years, I let go of my fear. Fear of what I *could* do. I gripped ahold of my internal flames, vowing that I wouldn't let them hurt Aspen.

Aspen who saw *me*. Saw my ugliness, saw the monster inside, knew what it had done, and wanted me still. Within her gaze, I found the part of me that was who I used to be. The Cole I was before the accident. The flicker of life inside me that I *liked* about myself. It was okay to be who I was. Half of one thing, and not quite all of another, the two halves of me, both phoenix and fire-drake made me who I was. I chose to be worthy of the trust she placed in me. Fledgling confidence settled in the flames racing through my core as my fear floated up, taking its choking hold with it.

So slowly I thought I might break from the wanting of it, I lowered my lips to hers. White hot fire danced across my lips, down my arms, blazed in my fingertips as I gripped her close.

I'd thought about it, dreamed about it, wanted it, but never thought it was within my grasp. Until now. Her lips burned in a way that I wanted to consume me. We bumped awkwardly together as we tried to find the way our lips best fit together. My knees went weak, and I wasn't sure live flames weren't bursting through my skin. Her mouth was cold against mine, fire and ice together and sending my head spinning. My hands wrapped around her middle, holding her close. Her fingers traced my jaw in a tingling trail of cold that sent a fresh wave of heat roiling through me.

And she was right. The hotter I burned, the colder she froze until a great cloud of steam enveloped us.

Our lips tangled together, frigid bursts against the lava inside me. A flash of heat surrounded by freeze. It was intoxicating. *Aspen* was intoxicating. My hands slid from her back to her sides. She reached up on tiptoe, her lips pressing harder against mine, and I was sure I'd combust.

We finally broke apart, steam pouring off us in all the places we touched. Flame and frost swirled together in a cloud of hazy, vaporous longing. For a long moment, we just stood there, searching the other's face, breathing harder than normal. Savoring what we'd just created together between the two of us. Aspen grasped the back of my head as she leaned her forehead against my shoulder.

My hand slid down her silky hair, and I leaned my ear against her head. My heart thrummed. Closing my eyes, I tried to memorize every thought and feeling pinwheeling through me.

"Cole!"

The urgency in her voice shook me from my memorization.

Suddenly fearful that I was hurting her, some latent reaction to my fire despite everything, I leaped back, knocking my head into the underside of the staircase.

She gripped my hand, and I breathed a sigh of relief as she looked at me, high color in her cheeks, but from the fire I'd kindled in her, not the fire of my skin.

Gingerly she reached out and grasped a tiny strand of magenta magic off my shoulder.

"Cole," she whispered. My mouth gaped.

"Where did that come from?" My voice was still rough, still completely affected by our kiss.

Aspen's eyebrows drew together. She looked around, and as she moved, I noticed the magenta dusting on her cheek like bright pink icing sugar.

"Aspen, you've got some more of the dust on your face." She stilled and let me brush my thumb over it. The steam still hanging around was damp enough that my thumb turned the dust into a smudge on her cheek.

"Oh, it prickles. Is it like the dust we found up in the tower?"

"Yeah." A thought was niggling at the back of my brain, trying to push itself through the haze of wonder that still drummed through me.

"Hold onto that string," Aspen said.

I had two seconds to tighten my grip on the filmy strand of magic before Aspen's lips were back on mine.

We kissed. I was pretty sure it was the best thing that had ever happened to me.

"Was there an ulterior motive for that?" I asked her, still a little breathless as she pulled back.

"Look at the magic." Her chest was still going up and down faster than normal, her eyes wide and animated as she tipped back far enough to look at me, her hand still braced against my bicep.

I glanced at the magic. My eyes bulged. It had *grown*.

It was easily twice the size it had been, its filmy gossamer surface sparkling like it was a newly minted coin, pulsing with its potential power.

"We made this." I heard the amazement in my own voice.

"We can go home." Aspen's words were hushed with wonder.

Our eyes met, unspoken excitement, fear, and trepidation flowing between us. But how could we leave now? Now that the Academy was at stake? Could we help win the battle we both knew was coming?

"We can't leave now," Aspen whispered.

"I know."

"So it is done."

Aspen yelped as together we startled and whirled towards a voice behind us for the second time that day.

"Alger-Aodh," I gasped.

The silvered head inclined gracefully towards us. Moonlight from the windows streamed in and lit his head with a halo-like glow. A puff of smoke erupted from his breast pocket and a tiny orange reptilian head poked out, his forked tongue flicking in and out.

"The time draws near." His deep draconic voice boomed in the quiet of the library.

"Time for what?" My heart was pounding, both from my recent encounter with Aspen's lips, the discovery of the magic, and now this. Alger-Aodh. Deep in my bones, I felt he somehow possessed the missing piece of the puzzle we needed.

A rueful smile graced the old man's lips. "Time. It is so fleeting, so enduring, so eternal. *Your time* is now upon you."

Aspen's hand tightened on the back of my shirt.

"Yours, too, little maiden of the ice," Alger-Aodh intoned with a sad twist of his lips.

Aspen let out a soft gasp behind me, her cool breath softly flitting against my ear.

The fire-drake's eyes smoldered with red coals, and for a moment, he seemed wreathed in bright translucent flames. Then he tipped his head up and slowly let his lids fall shut. The red glowed behind his paper-thin lids, giving him an ethereal appearance.

When he opened them and looked back at me, he was an impossibly tall elderly gentleman again. His eyes bored into mine. My heart hammered against my ribcage even as my tongue stuck to the roof of my mouth.

"You are a fire-drake at heart. Your mother gave fire to your eyes, flames to your soul, and flight to your spirit. But who you are—who you become, young drake—that is up to you. Your choices define you. Not your parentage, not your circumstances. Your choices. You must choose wisely and let *what* you were born aide you in *who* you become. It must be the way of things. Your fear is gone. Your way home is paved."

He stepped closer. Heat bled off him and my own rose, answering the call of the ancient's flames.

"Fly, fire-drake. Soar, phoenix." He bent towards me and gently blew a hot breath over me that sent heat rushing over every cell and left me quivering in anticipation. Aspen stepped back.

My chest expanded, my arms came out from my sides as fire, sweet, hot, and clean, burned through me, eating away my lingering doubts, washing me in a baptism of flames.

"The blessing is complete. I, too, am completed." Alger-Aodh stepped back and bowed once. With a flash, he was gone.

"Wait!"

Our breaths echoed in the large chamber of the library. My lungs ached, my fingers tingled, and my head spun.

"Cole?" Aspen's fingers tentatively ghosted against my shoulder. "What just happened?"

Meeting her worried eyes, my heart seemed to sprout its own wings.

"He...he..." How did I describe what had just happened to me? Looking down, I flexed my fingers. Fire ran contentedly below the surface. Scorching, powerful...and contained.

"I think he granted me complete control." Gratitude forced tears to my eyes and a lump to my throat.

"I think you were already on your way there. Maybe he just gave you the confidence to embrace it fully." Her eyes were clear and shining with pride as she stared up at me. A smile toyed with the corners of her lips.

My shoulders rose and fell with a deep breath. A breath weighted with promise, possibility, but not guilt. Not fear. Not anxiety.

"This is the first time in four years that I've felt *free*." I let the sensation linger.

This time when our lips met, there was no hesitation, there was no guilt, there was no fear. My fires were encased inside me, as they should be, while a different whiter, purer flame raced along my skin at Aspen's touch.

My fingers slid into her hair and cupped the back of her head. Her arms twined around my neck. We kissed slowly, savoring each sensation of lips meeting, quiet touches, still flame and still frost, but meeting gently, not in a clash of steam and passion.

We made our way back to the cottage sometime in the deep folds of night, the magenta magic tucked safely in Aspen's skirt pocket. Once the doors of the school shut behind us, a tangible force of fear seemed to wrap around me, stealing some of the confidence I'd built up over the course of the evening. The gravity of the coming battle weighed on me. Torches dotted the walls and in the windows of several huts, lights still shone from windows. Sentries walked the battlements up high on the thick walls that surrounded the Academy.

The hairs on the back of my neck raised and fire rushed through me in agitation. These people were spooked. And they were right to be. I wished I'd been able to hear more of Professor Rashtin's history lesson on the war before we'd inadvertently landed ourselves on the cusp of the battle. Aspen's chilly fingers trembled slightly against mine.

As quietly and quickly as we could, we unlocked the door and shut ourselves in the cottage. There was no sign of Jack or Anna Beth. They were probably long since in bed. Exhaustion ebbed the adrenaline from me as I locked the door. I stared at the metal lock for a minute. I touched it. It hadn't super-heated. Had hardly warmed up at all. A fatigued smile broke over my face.

"It's real, Cole. You have your control back," Aspen whispered tiredly, giving my arm a quick squeeze.

That night I stretched out on the pallet opposite Aspen's. I was asleep within minutes. Rest, deep, sweet, and easy, cocooned my body until the opening of a door had me cracking my eyes open.

We kissed.

CHAPTER 35

ASPEN

I woke slowly after a few hours of blissful sleep. Cole kissed me. I kissed him. It was literally magical. Magical enough we'd made a magenta strip of magic and a way to get back to our own time.

But that thought sobered me and brought me crashing back to reality and the looming confrontation with Lord Broderick's men.

Sitting up, I saw Jack tip toeing into the kitchen. "Jack?"

"Sorry to have awakened you. It's still quite early."

There were lines on his forehead. His eyes were red. Even his beard seemed droopy.

"Are you worried?"

He looked up at me. "Gravely."

Chills that had nothing to do with my ancestry shivered over me.

"We're going to stay to help." Cole rose up on his elbows.

Jack started in surprise. Probably because Cole was surrounded by a pile of flammable material.

"We met with Alger-Aodh last night as he requested. I can control it now." Cole's sleepy grin was wide enough it showed his white even teeth. He held up a hand to demonstrate, wiggling his fingers.

"Congratulations," Jack said, shadows cupping his eyes as he tried to lift his lips into a smile. "That's wonderful. And I get the feeling we could use all the help we can get." He stared at us a moment. I bit my lip, remembering he'd told us not to tell him things, even if he asked.

I met Cole's gaze across the room as Jack turned slowly to put the kettle on the stove.

My cheeks heated as a lazy smile drifted over Cole's face, amber flecks floating in his dark eyes. He had crazy wicked bed head after sleeping on a pillow. It made my toes curl. Suddenly, I was acutely aware of what my own hair must look like.

Fortunately, Anna Beth walked out of her room then, and I was spared additional embarrassment.

She frowned at us, her mouth a hard line, her eyes like blue flint. It was not the look of a friend. Without speaking to either of us, she went to slice bread at the wooden counter.

Cole lumbered from his bed and paced over to mine where he reached a hand down to help me up.

My mouth went dry, and heat curled in my middle as my palm slid into his.

His fingers grazed my waist once I was on my feet, and we moved to the table. Cole hesitated, carefully running a finger over the wooden surface, a look of awe stamped on his face.

"Has this been a ploy the whole time you've been here?" Anna Beth spat as Cole sank slowly onto a chair at the table.

"Peace, Anna Beth!" Jack said sternly.

"Well, look at him! He's sitting there at the table. Nothing burning to cinders and ash. He's been lying to us the entire time." The venom in her tone had my mouth hanging open in shock.

"Anna Beth, it's not like that at all." Cole stood, his hands in front of him trying to placate her anger. "I haven't lied to you about anything. I still have raging fires inside me, but Alger-Aodh did something to me last night. He said he finished the blessing. Somehow, he gave me back the control I've been missing for years. That's the only reason I'm able to sit at this table, or sleep on those blankets without this entire place going up in flames." Angry red sparks jumped in his eyes, not like the lazy amber ones when he looked at me.

My heart beat heavily against my ribs. I didn't know what to say to make this situation better. Tension crawled over my scalp and tightened in my shoulders. Anna Beth seemed determined to hate us.

Her chin quivered and without another word, she slammed the knife, point down, where it stuck quivering in the counter, and dashed out the front door.

"I'm sorry," Jack muttered as he jerked the knife out of the wood. "She does not handle pressure well. These new threats with Lord Broderick have put the entire Academy on edge. Anna Beth is feeling the strain most severely. We are all fearful of what may be coming."

Cole glanced at me. Nervously, I nodded.

"You should be." Cole's words crashed like weights down to the floor.

Jack's head snapped up with enough force his beard kept going once his head stopped.

"What do you mean?" The demand was clear in his voice.

"You need to send for reinforcements." Cole glanced at me again. I shrugged. In for a snowflake, in for a blizzard. Cole continued. "And speak to Alger-Aodh if you can. I think he has seen specific things regarding the war and what we should do. And he's going to be a pivotal part of what comes next."

Jack nodded. "I'll do it."

"Those men yesterday mentioned something below. Cole, I think we should check things out. I've been in some of the tunnels in our time. Maybe I'll see something that stands out," I said, running what we'd overheard over in my mind.

Jack nodded. "That would be helpful. I was going to amass a group to do a search, but if you can scour things this morning, if you see anything, that might give us more information as to where to concert our efforts. I'll still get a search party put together, but we'll plan to go down after the noon hour. Will that give you enough time?"

"It'll be enough time to at least do a quick sweep of the areas I'm familiar with." Hope fluttered in my chest that maybe we could do something helpful. I ignored the tingling in my chest that said maybe we'd be doing something condemning instead. It felt right, to stay and fight, rather than escape back to our time. I desperately hoped my gut was right. Because if it wasn't, our timeline might cease to exist.

"Good enough." Jack tugged his beard. "I will also ensure that a gryphon rider is sent out on the hour with news of the threat to King Trindon."

"Tell him to bring his army." Cole stood, serious and as immovable as a mountain of stone. Jack's already waxen face paled further at Cole's words.

"I know you told us not to tell you what is coming, but in this case, I think we'd be stupid not to," Cole explained. I nodded. That feeling of *rightness* settled in my belly.

"Perhaps you have been sent here just for this occasion." Jack stared at us for a moment. Then, with a little bow of reverence that sent shock waves rippling to my toes, Jack straightened, grabbed a piece of bread and slathered some honey on it. "I'm going to get to work on things now. I'll gather a group and see if I can track down Alger-Aodh. Shall we reconvene at noon here to discuss what you've found and where we should best concentrate our efforts?"

I nodded.

"Will you be needing a torch for the tunnels?" Jack asked, an eyebrow raised.

Cole grinned. "Nope."

We borrowed some long cloaks, and with the hoods up, we made it into the Academy without drawing unwanted attention. There was plenty of confusion and chaos to provide us with enough diversion to avoid detection. We went down the hall past the main office and took the one that branched out from the cloisters. Tucked away neatly at the side of the end of the hall was a brass-bound door, heavy oaken slats already turning a rich dark brown with age.

With a groan of protest, the door opened, and we stood at the top of a long black staircase. I shivered as a gust of damp, dank air rushed to greet us.

"Homey place," Cole quipped. His nose wrinkled at the smell of *old wet* wafting up from the depths below the Academy. "Time for a fireball." Cole's deep voice, though only at a whisper, echoed slightly against the stone walls. I suppressed another shiver.

"Need ice?" I asked.

"Not for this anymore. But I think I'll be needing ice in my life for a long time."

A plume of flame the size of a cantaloupe erupted and hovered over his palm, illuminating his cheeky grin. My lips tugged upwards as little flurries of tingling flittered through me. I pulled the heavy door the rest of the way shut.

"I know we have a fast-approaching deadline and need to get searching, but I'd really like to kiss you first. You know...for luck?" His smile turned shy.

He moved closer, his arm brushing against mine, his hand held out away from us, creating an intimate circle of light around us.

"We could probably use all the luck we could get," I offered. My voice had a breathless quality to it that seemed to happen anytime Cole got within kissing distance.

"I agree."

Cole closed his palm and the light winked out, leaving us in darkness. I could see amber flecks floating in his eyes amidst the blackness.

"I'm in control, but I still don't want to risk singeing your hair with open flames."

I was going to respond with some witty retort, but it flew out of my head as his hand sought mine in the dark, trailed up my arm, over my shoulder, my neck, found my jaw, and slid into my hair. His other hand reached out and caught my shoulder before cupping the other side of my face.

My hands found his elbows and worked up to his shoulders as his lips closed softly over mine.

He tasted like heat, cinnamon, and smoke. I pressed closer to him, and the pads of his fingers brushed lightly over my cheeks. His heart beat hard enough I could feel it against my own chest.

A little gasp escaped without my permission.

Cole groaned against my lips.

"I'm going to need that ice after all if you keep making noises like that," he mumbled against my lips.

A giggle worked its way up my throat.

"Maybe you need more exposure, you know, become more desensitized to it," I teased as his thumb swept the line of my jaw.

"Yeah. I don't think that's ever going to happen. I'm pretty sure I could kiss you over and over and never get tired of it. But I'm more than happy to practice more exposure. Anytime."

He gently kissed the tip of my nose, somehow finding it in the dark without missing. Maybe his phoenix eyes saw better in the blackness than mine did. Snow swirled in my middle, contentment and excitement thrumming through me.

"That's good. Because I *really* like it when you kiss me." I kissed him softly on the lips once more before leaning back. "As much as I'd love to stand here and kiss you until noon, we should take a look around."

Cole sighed. "I know." Flames sprung to life once more, cradled in his palm. "See any more of our magic?"

A shiver worked its way over my spine at the way he said *our magic*.

"Hold the fire up higher." As he did, I spotted a string of magenta clinging to my shirt. I picked it up, folded it a few times, then stuck it in the pocket of Anna Beth's skirt that desperately needed to be laundered.

"You know, before we leave, we should probably make a lot more of those strands," Cole said, a contemplative look crossing his face.

"Oh?" A smile crept into my voice.

"If there aren't surviving magenta strands from now, back in our time, we won't ever be able to get back here. We might never otherwise kiss. And I don't want to miss out on that."

"Wow. I hadn't gotten there yet, but you're right." I smiled despite the sobering thought. "I don't want to miss out on kissing you either. And you'd never meet Alger-Aodh, never get your fire-drake blessing, and would probably have to spend a lot longer learning to control your flames."

"Probably. And I'm grateful for all of those things. But I never want to forget this." He held up our twined hands.

I lifted our knot of fingers and kissed the back of his hand. "Me neither."

He blew a hard breath out his mouth.

"Okay. We should keep moving and focus before I stop for more exposure."

Chuckling, we set off down the dark hallway into the unknown blackness of the underground portion of the Academy.

Not only was it dark, the deeper we went, the damper it became. Little drips slid down the walls at intervals and some patches had little fuzzy green bits clinging to the walls.

"We should tell Jack someone needs to come down here and look at these foundations. It's not wet like this in our time. I mean, it's not like a five-star resort, but it's dry." I frowned at the drips and wondering about crumbling and all the tons of rock above us.

"I have no idea what that guy at the river thought was below the school, because we haven't seen anything other than what feels like miles of tunnels. Why are all these even down here?" Cole let his flames jump higher and illuminated the corridor until it went around a bend.

My lips pursed as my forehead wrinkled. "I feel like we must be missing something. Maybe something obvious. But other than a trickle of water down the walls here and there, I haven't seen any openings to the outside world anywhere. I have no idea how someone would get down here, from out there." My arm waved in the general direction of the hallway.

"So we go back and tell Jack we found nothing?"

"I guess so. It's probably close to time for us to head back anyway."

Cole sighed. "I was hoping we'd find something wildly helpful down here."

"Me, too."

Cole squeezed my hand. "Any chance of one more bit of exposure before we go back?" Amber drifted in his irises and made my insides melt.

Instead of answering him, I grinned at him from beneath my lashes. My fingers found his shoulders, and the light went out as his hands lightly brushed my waist.

Before his lips could touch mine, a whispered brush of conversation hit my sensitive ears. I jerked my head to the side. Shivering as Cole's warm lips grazed the side of my neck, I blinked into the darkness, straining my ears.

There.

The faintest stirrings of words. I brought my hand up and covered Cole's mouth. He kissed my palm and pulled back. Taking my hand from his mouth, I left one finger so he knew to be quiet.

Sparks flared to life in his palm, and without thought, I covered it with mine, sending a quick shower of snow over the sparks.

I could feel his confusion in the darkness. His body went taut as the softly echoing words ricocheted down the hallway. His hand tightened on mine. Without words, we crept to the end of the passage.

Poking my ear around the side of the stone and into the main corridor, the words came louder. Still too soft to be understood, but they were clearly coming from the left branch of the hallway—away from the entrance back into the Academy.

A quick tug on Cole's hand and we moved silently as wraiths down the hallway towards the voices. As we moved, the voices became clearer. One was raised in anger, the other wavering with concern.

"You said the entrance would be ready by tonight."

"I can't help that the fire-drake set up camp right where we need to dig! Besides," the voice took on a whining quality, "you have the other entrance. It's small, but you can get inside the walls."

"I can't march an army against this place by infiltrating underground one man at a time. They'll pick us off like pixies."

"Then I'll need more time."

"You have no more time. Lord Broderick is ready to move. The planets are aligned in our favor one night hence. We will attack at dawn. You must have the secondary entrance completed. The main force will march on the main gate, but I want an entrance big enough for three hundred men to come through quickly."

"Three hundred will be more than enough to completely subdue this place. Why so big a force?"

"Lord Broderick wants it razed to the ground. I carry out my orders. There is too much free magic in this place. It will have too many consequences. We must destroy it. The hybrids being bred here are creating new magic the world has never seen. That is dangerous. Its price will mark our children's children."

My blood iced solid in my veins. This was it. It wasn't about control of the magic—not even about the freedom to use it; it was fear of it. Fear of...hybrids? And the magic they produced? Hybrid species were as common in our time as snowflakes in a blizzard. But aside from that, there was a traitor in our midst, and somehow, they had found a way to smuggle the enemy inside Magik Prep. Even more than that, there was an army somewhere out there, ready to fall upon the school and decimate it.

Cole's hand tightened around mine. He squeezed three times. I hoped I interpreted the pressure of his hand correctly.

I squeezed back. We squeezed together. One. Two. *Three*!

On three, Cole threw a fireball down the hallway. It kept us hidden in shadows but illuminated the dull stones, and two men standing down the length of the corridor.

"We're found!" the whiny voice screeched.

The scrape of steel on scabbard set my teeth on edge and my heart hammering in my throat.

With a grunt, Cole pummeled another fireball in their direction, high enough it wouldn't burn them. I followed the trajectory of his flames with two streaks of ice.

Two cries let me know I'd found my mark.

"Let me out!"

Steel chipped away at the block of ice I'd formed around the taller man's feet. He'd be free in minutes.

"Light!" I called to Cole.

Both his hands blazed to life, columns of flame shooting off his hands. A hasty glance at his face let me know he was still fully in control, but sweet snowfall, did he ever cut an imposing figure with his twin pillars of flame illuminating his burnished hair and glinting on the golden pieces, his squared jaw set, his eyes black and dangerous.

I quickly looked back to the two men, both partially encased in ice, the taller fiercer one hacking away at it with his sword. With another frigid inhale, I let the ice fly from my fingers, solidifying the quickly crumbling block and encasing the man up to his thighs. He howled in frustration, squirming in his freezing prison.

"Drop your sword." Cole's fire-drake side was evident in the way his voice reverberated in my bones and down the stone walls. Flames lashed his eyes, making the whiny man at the end of the hall tremble against his frozen bonds. The taller man, belligerent and uncowed, scowled and gripped his sword tighter.

"No." The word dripped with malice.

Cole was unfazed. "You drop it, or I'll make you."

"No, you won't. You're a sniveling rodent, unworthy of standing before me." The tall man spat.

Cole raised an eyebrow, totally nonplused. It infuriated the taller man.

In a display of control that I would have thought beyond most our age, Cole expanded the plume of fire in his left hand and extinguished the column in his right. With the precision of an expert marksman, Cole pointed one finger and sent a white-hot stream of fire streaking to the man's sword.

The sword turned red within seconds.

With a shout the man dropped it and waved his smoking hand before holding it flat against the ice on his legs. Cole withdrew his heat while I sent a hefty wave of ice over the sword, making a solid mound of freeze that no bare fingers could claw through.

"Go get Jack," Cole told me. My belly clenched. I didn't want to leave Cole down here by himself with the two men, and honestly, I didn't want to go back up to the Academy through those dark tunnels by myself either. I swallowed.

"Quickly, Aspen," he said softly. I heard the urgency in his voice, felt it in my toes. We were on a deadline. Lord Broderick's men were in the vicinity, and not only the Academy and our lives were at stake, but our entire way of life in the future hinged on the outcome of the coming battle.

My teeth rattled as I suddenly realized just how much was riding on our shoulders at this very second.

"I'll hurry," I whispered. "You're good?"

A dark half smile lifted Cole's cheek. "Oh, I'm good. Because," he raised his voice, "if either of these two morons so much as flinches, I'll incinerate them."

The smaller man whimpered. The taller glared daggers at Cole, but kept his mouth shut.

"All right. Be careful." I quickly kissed his cheek.

"For luck?" He winked.

"For luck." My smile was wobbly.

"I'll hold the flames as high as I dare to give you as much light as possible."

"Okay. This tunnel goes straight up to the door and opens onto the main floor of the Academy. Even if I can't see, I should still be able to get back so long as I don't make any turns."

"I'll see you soon."

With another nod, I fled up the hallway until all Cole's light had faded, and darkness crowded around me.

Once completely entombed in the inky blackness, I let my fingers graze the side of the wall. I was high enough up that at least they were dry and no slimy gunk coated the rocks. Urgency pounded through my veins, and fear for Cole had my feet going as fast as I dared in the blackness. I didn't have to go terribly far before a thin strip of light appeared and with a sigh of relief, I realized it was the crack of light from the door into the Academy proper.

Hesitating a moment before the door, I debated with myself. It was the middle of the day. I sighed. Realizing the time for stealth and keeping our presence a secret was over, I shoved open the door and strode boldly down the hallway.

Students stared as I ran the length of the corridor, white-blonde hair flying behind me, Anna Beth's dirty skirt clenched in my fists and showing an appreciable length of my legs. I ignored the catcalls from the bolder students and the shocked gasps from most as I heaved the door open and sprinted towards the cottage.

I rolled my eyes, thinking how similar my last experience was in my own time in that same hallway. Wretched rumors.

Weak sunlight filtered down, though I hardly noticed. Bursting through the cottage door, I startled Jack and the cluster of older creatures gathered around him. He dropped the charcoal stick he was holding on top of the sprawling map spread over the table.

"Aspen! What's wrong?"

"Jack, we found a traitor and one of Lord Broderick's men. Cole has them cornered in the tunnels. We have to go *now*."

CHAPTER 36

COLE

I didn't have to wait long. Probably only fifteen or twenty minutes after Aspen left, footsteps echoed down the hallway behind me. Neither of the men trapped in Aspen's ice had said a word. We'd stared at each other as my flames flickered against the blackness.

"Cole?" Aspen's voice filtered down the hallway and my shoulders lost some of their rigid tenseness.

"We're all still here. Who's with you?" I called back.

"Jack, and several other members of the board who happened to be close at hand."

Glancing back, my shoulders relaxed a fraction more, unconsciously tight in her absence. Jack's head bobbed right behind her, and several other weathered faces in varying shapes and sizes came behind him.

One of the board members sporting pointed ears and webbed fingers gasped and clutched at her chest.

"Brutus!" she murmured. What a fitting name for a traitor.

The smaller man with the whiny voice hung his head, slumping as he could in his ice encasement.

"Why would you do this?" another board member asked into the silence.

Brutus did not answer.

An hour later, Aspen and I were sitting back at Jack's having a late lunch. I was starving after keeping my fires going all morning. A smile flitted over my face as I sat on a wooden chair, my hand resting on the wooden tabletop. Jack and the board members had taken over care of the prisoners as soon as we were back in the Academy and there was light enough for me to douse my flames. They'd dragged the prisoners to parts unknown and Aspen and I had been directed back to the cottage.

"What do you suppose they're doing right now?" Aspen asked as she moved a few peas around on her plate.

"I hope the prisoners are spilling their guts and giving away all sorts of helpful information." I drained the water from my cup.

"Do you think we are—or will—change things by staying here to help?" Aspen worried her lip.

"I don't know," I told her honestly. The thought had crossed my mind. "I feel strongly that we're supposed to be here." I did. I felt it in my fire gut. "But I don't want to do something that's going to upset the balance of things back in our time either. I don't know the difference between sense and wisdom there," I admitted.

"Do you think we should tell Jack everything we know? I mean, we know what we learned in history class, but since we've been here, we also know that it's not entirely correct. There is no glacier for Alger-Aodh to melt. There is no Chasm yet, and I'm at a loss as to how it's formed. Several of the pieces from our history classes are missing here. I don't know what's real and what's been lost over the past however many hundreds of years. I'm afraid of saying something that will change too much. But I'm afraid to leave them on their own here, too, at the mercy of Lord Broderick, for fear that we *won't* do something we're supposed to and that will change the future, too."

A knock sounded at the door before I could reply. The hairs on the back of my neck stood on end as Aspen's eyes went wide.

"It's Duri!" a muffled voice came through the door.

"Duri?" I whispered.

Aspen raised an eyebrow. "Duri. He of the leg ogling when we first dropped into the courtyard."

"Oh yeah." Blood rushed through me at the thought as needless jealousy reared its head.

He knocked again.

"Oh, for the love of ice," Aspen muttered.

I stood as Aspen stalked to the door and cracked it open a sliver.

"I'm so glad you're still here!" Duri said excitedly.

"What do you want?" Aspen asked.

"What do I want? Do you jest? You're from the future! You can help us out of this mess!"

"Oh, sweet snowfall," Aspen mumbled.

I was at her side in a second. My stomach dropped. Behind Duri were at least two dozen students. All with expressions ranging from hopeful to outright panic.

"No use in trying to hide now they've found us and word is out." I swung the door open fully, my fingers resting possessively against Aspen's back.

"Well, tell us what we need to do to beat these base-born sons of jackals!"

"Yes, help us!"

"What can we do?" The voices all shouted over each other, concern, anger, and panic coming at us in a confusing swirl of noise.

"They can't tell you anything. They are the reason Lord Broderick's men are coming here at all!" The words cut through the din like fire through ice.

My eyes swung around the crowd until I found Anna Beth. She stood a few paces away from the group, her arms crossed tightly across her chest. Murderous rage was stamped on her face.

Duri's expression fell.

"That cannot be. They've come back to help us. Haven't you?" He turned his broad brown eyes at us.

"We are not the cause of this trouble." Aspen projected her voice so that it rang out in the yard. "Lord Broderick has done that all on his own. But we *are* here to help you. *Our* leaders are right now dealing with two prisoners we captured this morning in the tunnels underneath the school."

Anna Beth's scowl deepened, and a few errant ice crystals escaped from her fingers where they were clenched tight across her chest. I nudged Aspen's back. She was doing a great job. The crowd was hanging on her every word. All save Anna Beth. She gave us a dark look that I'm pretty sure was meant to call down lightning from on high and obliterate us on the spot.

"You all are fools to listen to them." Bitterness and an undercurrent of terror leaked into Anna Beth's words.

"And you're a fool not to." The words escaped my mouth before I thought them all the way through. But they were out. I couldn't call them back now. Only way to go was forward. The crowd stared between me and Anna Beth. Her rage darkened. Students started moving subtly, towards Anna Beth or towards Duri.

"We *are* from the future. And there is a war coming. It's coming soon." Gasps echoed loud enough they bounced off the stone walls. Aspen reached back and found my hand. "I don't say it to scare you. But you need to be prepared."

"How do we prepare?" a voice called out.

"How many of you have internal magic?" Aspen asked.

Murmurs rumbled through the crowd.

"I do." A stalwart centaur stepped forward, arms crossed over a thick chest. He was so short and so wide he could have been part dwarf.

"What can you do?" I asked.

"I can direct my magic wherever I want it to go. I never miss."

"Too bad your magic is harmless!" someone near Anna Beth flung. The centaur flinched, a crack in his confident facade.

"Can you direct someone else's magic?" Aspen said. She took a step forward. The weak sunlight hit her pale skin, making her shimmer.

The centaur cocked his head to the side. "I think so? I've never tried."

A slow smile spread over Aspen's face. "I'm going to throw a snowball at you. I want you to direct it."

The centaur stood up taller, barrel chest puffing out. "Aye. Where do you want it to go?"

Aspen scanned the crowd and the wall some fifty feet or so to our right. "Can you hit that grey stone right at the top of the wall?"

"Undoubtedly." The confident swagger was back in the face of Aspen's challenge and an eager audience.

"Here we go." Aspen spun her wrist and a plump fluffy snowball appeared on her hand. Bringing her arm back in a motion that would make baseball players in our time envious, she let the snowball fly straight at the centaur's head.

He was startled, not expecting the snowball to move quite so rapidly, but recovered with enough time to send a wave of dark purple magic spangling from his finger. It wrapped around half the snowball, and the white fluff broke in half. Immediately, part of it changed its trajectory. The partial snowball impacted with such force that the dull *thunk* echoed down the walls. White encrusted the target stone. And the centaur's red face.

"Shall we try again?" Aspen said kindly, excitement and hope sparking in her blue eyes.

"Aye. I shan't miss any this time," the centaur said, dark brows drawn low in concentration.

Aspen let another snowball fly.

Ready for it this time, the purple magic spiraled out, circling the whole snowball and flinging it with another *thunk* into the target stone.

"Excellent," Aspen praised as she dusted her hands together. "Think you can do that with a weapon?"

"Now that I know what to expect, it should be easy enough to hit the target every time," he said with a wide grin.

"That's the sort of thing we should be preparing to do. Back in our time, they teach us these things in a basic magic defense class. We're going to do that now." Aspen's voice rang with finality. "Find your friends. Find creatures with magic that is compatible with yours, or with magic you can manipulate. Strategize with each other. Let's start by grouping together in ways that will be helpful in keeping the enemy away from the walls and out of Magik Prep."

I stared at Aspen. Whether she realized it or not, she had just given these students a purpose and hope that they could do something useful to ensure their own survival. Hope—powerful and tangible—tingled in my chest.

Jack and the other school leaders exited the building about two hours later as the sun was considering its descent. Jack's weathered face elongated as his mouth dropped open, his beard dusting the third button down on his shirt. He searched the crowd and met my gaze. Jack's blue eyes drew life and bloomed with wary excitement as he nodded once to me then took in the students in various stages of practicing defensive magic.

His back stiffened as he saw Anna Beth leaning belligerently against a tree. She and several other students grouped about her watched us. The scowl never left her face. Jack walked towards the tree.

Anna Beth's scowl turned into a snarl as her father approached. Pulling my eyes from what was sure to be an uncomfortable encounter, I gazed back at the students practicing their defensive magic.

Strands of colored magic littered the ground around the students. Combining their magic was producing great heaps of the stuff. This section of the school grounds was starting to take on a distinctly modern look with all the magic floating around.

Aspen snatched a strand of orange magic and bent it absently in her fingers as she sauntered back over to where I stood at the edge of the path.

"My internal magic is light blue. Yours is hot pink, isn't it." It was a statement, not a question, as a hidden smile curled one corner of her mouth upward.

"Variations of it, depending on my mood, yes," I answered, curious to what she was thinking. My father's internal magic was deep red. My mother, as a phoenix, was bright white.

She looked up at me, awe written on her face. "We make magenta magic together. Look at all these pieces of magic that are all over the place now. What do you notice?"

I surveyed the students, still practicing, still exploding random bursts of colors as magic was combined, shared, stretched, and used. Magic fluttered on the breeze. Orange. Green. Purple. Pink. Opalescent. Grey.

"It's the combinations. That's it, isn't it?" I turned to her, excitement brimming as understanding dawned.

"Yeah. I think so. Lord Broderick is right to fear the hybrids. Look what we're doing. Internal magic is always a variant of red, blue, yellow, white, or black. All these other color combinations—they're formed with hybrid magic. Look at Johnny—the centaur? He makes dark purple magic. I'd bet next year's snowfall that his parents weren't the same race. Red blooded centaur and dark blooded dwarf?"

A surprised chuckle bubbled up my throat.

"And there's been little to no magic laying around like there is in our time. You have to be right. It is the hybrids—and the hybrid magic that gives—or at least will give—Magik Prep the edge. Why it will survive." I shook my head in wonder and new appreciation at what was unfolding before us.

"Our differences are our strengths when we work together and combine them." She laced her fingers with mine.

A smile lifted the corners of my mouth. My differences were my strengths. Alger-Aodh had confirmed as much in different words. Adrenaline still thrummed through my veins, but a certain peace had descended despite it. Fire gurgled happily in my belly.

"I see you both have been active in my absence." Jack gave a little laugh as he joined us on the path. He scanned the students and the filmy strands of magic accruing haphazardly with an expression of awe.

"Did you find out anything else with your...interrogation?" I asked.

"Brutus told us everything he knows. Which isn't terribly much." Jack's face was pained, as was the sigh that let loose as his shoulders fell. "Lord Broderick's man though, he's a vault. Would say nothing."

Aspen looked at me before turning to Jack.

"In our history class back in our time, we were beginning to discuss this battle that's coming," Aspen hedged.

Jack's head snapped up, all his attention riveted on her. Aspen glanced at me. I nodded, my hand skimming her arm in encouragement. Silently, we agreed to lay all our cards on the table.

"Given the circumstances, I think it would be best if we told you everything we know. I'm not sure how much of it is exactly accurate, but I think it may be safer for us to share all the information we have."

Jack nodded with a heavy sigh. "Let's get the rest of the board. We'll meet back in my cottage."

CHAPTER 37

ASPEN

The door shut behind us, and we were mercifully alone for a few moments. I needed to collect myself. I'm not sure what came over me when I found Duri on the stoop. I was nervous and fearful. But when Anna Beth accused us of being at fault for the trouble waiting somewhere out beyond the walls, something snapped inside me.

And now I might have introduced the very beginnings of the Academy's magic defense classes.

I snorted.

"What is it?" Cole took my hands and led me away from the door to the middle of the room. I leaned my head against his shoulder as his hands wrapped comfortingly around me.

"Just realizing that I may have created the beginnings of the defense courses I took in our time—the stuff I encouraged everybody out there to do—it's all stuff I learned from that class. What if I'm the creator of that class?" My eyebrows drew together. "All this time traveling, going around in circles, makes my head hurt."

His laughter rumbled in his chest as his hand stroked over my hair.

"Still think we're giving them too much information? Or you think this is for the best?" His deep voice vibrated my ear as it pressed against him.

I breathed in his smoky cinnamon smell. "I wish I knew. We stayed because we wanted to ensure that the battle has the right outcome. Now that it's coming, I feel like we've locked ourselves into something that we think is true...but we're not absolutely, one-hundred percent sure of it."

His hand ran over my hair again. "I think we should lay out everything we know and see what the leaders think."

"What if Anna Beth is right?" I whispered.

"About what?" His fingers played with the ends of my hair.

"What if they are all fools for following us. What if we do upset the balance, or somehow caused Lord Broderick to attack now?" Dread grew in a lump in my middle.

Cole was still for a minute while his thumb drew maddeningly pleasant circles on my right shoulder blade. "I'm not any better with this time travel stuff, but we do know that in our time, the battle happened. Whether with or without us, it happened. If we're the cause, or the outcome, we're here now. And it already happened in our time. So, it stands to reason, that whatever we do here, will generate the same history." He stilled a minute. "I hope."

I wrapped my arms tighter around him, wanting to feel the solid warmth of his presence and let it ground me.

He kissed the tip of my pointed ear and whispered, "We'll make it. Magik Prep will make it, too."

I tipped my head back for a proper kiss, but the creak of the door handle doused that idea. I stepped back, but not completely. Cole's hand drifted down my arm and caught my fingers as Jack and several other grey heads spilled into the room.

Swirls of magic clung to a few of them, and I found that it buoyed my spirits and renewed my sense of purpose in telling them everything.

Jack made introductions.

"I could not find Alger-Aodh," Jack's voice and eyes held his regret.

"He must know we're in dire need," a plump elf with exorbitantly long ears said.

"He's going to be important to the plan, too," Cole said.

I squeezed Cole's hand and addressed the group. "If he sees glimpses of the future, I'm sure he knows where and when he's needed." I glanced at Jack for confirmation. Jack nodded uncertainly. Tendrils of doubt wormed their way into my belly. What if our history had everything wrong? Dread surfaced again, threatening to sink its claws into my chest.

Cole's fingers suddenly spasmed around mine hard enough it hurt.

Grunting, he dropped my hand and gripped his head.

"Cole?" I heard the worry in my own voice.

He dragged in a lung full of air. Looking up, soft noises of shock rippled around those gathered. Cole's eyes were bright orange—a hue I'd never seen in them. My heart hammered against my chest. What was happening to Cole? Was he hurt? Were his flames going to incinerate the lot of us? Terror coated my tongue and dried my throat. Ice prickled at the tips of my fingers.

As quickly as it had come, it left. Cole's chest heaved. Mine did, too. My hand instinctively clutched at my shirt where my heart was thumping hard enough the cotton material quivered.

"Sorry," he panted. "I don't know what happened." He shook his head like a dog flinging off water droplets. "That was like a power surge or something."

"Your mark is glowing," I whispered. I pulled in a breath and willed my heart to slow.

"He's been blessed by the fire-drake," someone said softly.

Our group took on a new air of reverence towards Cole. Where before they had been curious and desperate, maybe dubious, the atmosphere now felt tinged with respect and hope. Cole reached for my hand again. It was warmer than his new normal. I sent a little wave of cold traveling up his arm and his shoulders relaxed a fraction. My heart rate slowed, no longer pounding with enough force to burst through my ribs.

"Here's what we know," Cole soldiered on ahead as if nothing had happened though trepidation still lingered, coiled in my back. "Our history records that there was a giant glacier that Alger-Aodh blasted into a torrent of water that flooded into what we call the Chasm—a deep gorge that the river runs through—and stranded Lord Broderick's army on an island in the middle of the water until King Trindon's forces were able to come and take care of them."

Slight frowns and puzzled expressions met Cole's words.

"I'm unclear what this means for us now," a matronly fae said as she tapped a finger against her red lips.

"That's part of the problem. So are we," I interjected. "In our time, there is an island—roughly where the mountain is now. But we were taught that there was a glacier that was melted. There is no glacier—only the river. Is there any hidden ice underground, a cave system? Or in the mountain itself that our history could have originated from?"

"Ice, no. But you said yourself, there's the river. It surrounds the mountain on three sides." Jack looked hard at me and the wheels in my head started turning frantically.

The river. The Chasm. The glacier.

I gasped.

My hand flew to my mouth.

Maybe instigating magic defense classes weren't the only thing I would put in motion while in this time.

"We could make the ice." The whispered words dropped from my mouth like an icicle shattering on the ground.

Why had I not considered it before?

Jack nodded, his blue eyes dancing with excitement.

"We could freeze the river. Send the ice down into the ground so that..." My words drifted off and I stared at Cole.

"You made the Chasm," he finished for me.

I blinked stupidly as awareness crashed down. Shaking my head, I refused to dwell on the impact that I would have both on this time and my time and plunged on ahead.

"Jack, you can shoot ice down into the ground, right? Displace the earth?" It was such a simple solution. I did it when I was frustrated. I released the tension straight into the ground as shards of ice. But if the shards of ice were big enough, and we expanded and froze the river, too, that would definitely make cracks big enough to form the basis of the Chasm around the mountain.

"Of course. You're thinking surround them on all sides, ice them in and then melt it, so the troops are stranded on the mountain-turned-island?" Jack's beard quivered in his enthusiasm.

I nodded, my own excitement rising. This could work. This could really work! History said it did. I fervently hoped that history was correct.

"Are there any other creatures here who can make ice?"

Jack's face shuttered. "Only Anna Beth." He looked solemnly at Cole and me, meeting both our eyes. "I will speak to her. Make her see reason."

A clamor outside the cottage made me twitch. Cole wrapped an arm around me as a faun that looked suspiciously like an exceedingly young Professor Capra from our time opened the door.

"He's dead! He's gone!" the faun babbled.

"Who?" Jack asked, his bushy eyebrows shooting up his forehead in concern.

"Alger-Aodh. The great fire-drake is dead! He's been murdered!"

CHAPTER 38

COLE

My blood froze. Then a wave of heat so intense it made Aspen flinch beside me, flooded every vein in my body.

I gasped for air.

Aspen sent a wave of cold shooting up my arm that helped calm some of the rush of emotion hurtling through me.

Alger-Aodh was dead? Murdered? Who? Where? Why? How? How could someone possibly get the upper hand on a future-seeing fire-drake?

And why was I having such an intense reaction? Mentally and emotionally, I was sad—he'd helped me. He was an ancestor who had come to mean surprisingly much in just a few interactions. But I was having a physical reaction I couldn't control.

Parts of my body were spasming, like tiny volcanos going off in random places inside me.

"Don't let go," I whispered to Aspen as a swirl of concern, grief, and shock rose from those gathered around us.

"I won't." Another wave of cold rocketed up my arm and I sucked in another lungful.

Alger-Aodh was dead.

He was supposed to hold off the enemy army until King Trindon's troops got here.

I groaned and let my head sink into my free hand. Suddenly, I knew exactly how someone could get the upper hand on a future-seeing fire-drake. He let them.

His blessing. It wasn't about giving me back my control. I saw things clearly—perhaps for the first time. I'd done that on my own. Alger-Aodh's blessing had been the excuse I'd needed to stand on my own two feet. To master and control my fear. But the blessing. It had been the passing of Alger-Aodh's legacy. I felt it now. Deep in my bones, in my fire belly as smoke filled my fire lung, ready to heave the pent-up flames at my command.

Alger-Aodh knew he was going to die. He'd intentionally passed his legacy to me before his time came. He'd seen this whole future.

"Cole?" Aspen's concerned face swam into focus. I swallowed hard as responsibility rested on my shoulders like a heavy cloak.

"I'm the fire-drake. The one from the legend." Terror and wonder flooded my system, making me dizzy. "He passed his blessing—his mantle—on to me that night in the library. He knew he was going to die. He knew I'd be the only fire-drake left at the Academy. 'I am completed,' he said."

"Sweet snowfall. Professor Rashtin said it was one of the greatest fire-drakes known to history. Cole, you're massive. You are covered in fire—you breathe it, you can shoot it from your eyeballs. Your wings and tail are always lit. This world has never seen a fire-drake like you. For all we know, the world will never see another one like you again. I mean, you're pretty awesome for other reasons, too," she broke off with a nervous giggle as the vastness of what we were meant to do settled in. "Oh, wow, this is all happening fast." Her bottom lip tucked in between her teeth.

"Seriously." My voice was breathless. Alger-Aodh wasn't going to be the one to keep the enemy army at bay or melt the frozen river. It was me.

"What do we do now?" a voice in the background asked.

Half a dozen sets of eyes were suddenly on Aspen and me as the adults in the room looked to us for guidance. I'd never felt so inadequate before in all my life. My gulp was audible. Several of the women in the room dabbed at their eyes with sleeves or hankies.

"I am part fire-drake." I announced and swallowed hard again. "I think I'm the one our history class spoke of. I can melt the frozen river to strand Lord Broderick's men."

"You can fly?"

"Breathe fire?"

"Are you certain?"

"You're so young!"

All the voices echoed between my ears, making me wince. I lacked enough confidence to do this as it was. It was one thing telling everybody what I learned in history class. To realize such a heavy responsibility had been passed on to me by the most famous fire-drake in recorded antiquity. It was another to be thrust into the role you thought would be filled by that most famous fire-drake. Hearing the doubts of the Academy leaders was doing nothing for my confidence.

"Yes. To all of it." Aspen's words carried a finality that dared anyone to challenge them. My heart sputtered at her confidence in me.

A horn blasted outside on the walls.

We were out of time. The enemy had been sighted.

CHAPTER 39

ASPEN

Dawn light scraped grey fingers across the bottom of the rim of sky out in the distance. My heart thundered with dread, anticipation, and not a small measure of disbelief.

There, on the horizon behind the mountain, little black figures marched. The bald mountain top provided stark relief in the greying light as Lord Broderick's men marched to their battle lines. We needed to move.

My eye snagged on the mode of transportation that would take me to the far side of the river where I'd plunge my ice so deep that the heart of the earth cracked open a fissure that would strand an army. My mouth dried at the thought. My heart pumped loud enough Cole probably heard it as I stared at the glossy flanks, the curved talons, the massive wings, the wickedly curved beak.

A gryphon.

It's not like I hadn't seen them in my own time. I had friends in the gryphon riders program. They trained to ride and after graduation, if they continued on, they usually became part of the border patrollers. But I'd never personally ridden one of the furry, feathery beasts. Nor did I have a desire to.

I was almost as nervous about getting where I needed to go on gryphon back as I was actually doing what needed to be done.

"You sure you're okay?" Cole's hand palmed the small of my back as he came up beside me. He swallowed the last of the nuts he'd been eating. He was building up as much reserve fuel as he could.

"Yes?" It came out as a question.

Cole gave a mirthless chuckle as his fingers nudged me closer, so my side was flush against his.

"Are you?" I whispered, looking at his face. His eyes were troubled, his brows drawn close together under the golden ends of his hair.

"I'm less concerned about me than I am about you." He turned to face me fully. The amber sparks were swirling typhoons, not their usual lazy eddies. "You'll be out there." He waved his arm at the army. "I feel like I need to be with you. I have this insane urge to protect you. The thought of you going out there without me is making me crazy." He swiped a hand frustratedly through his hair.

The thing was, I knew exactly what he meant. I wanted him with me, too. Not because I couldn't take care of myself, but because we were better together. And if something happened to me, Cole could never get home. Or vice versa. But we both agreed that the ideal of Magik Prep—that all races be free to come to gather, to learn, to better each other by being *together*—was more important than us getting back to our own time.

"How about you?" I smoothed a piece of bronzy-gold hair back into place.

"I have the easy job."

I gave a half grin. "Sure."

"No, really. All I have to do is distract them while you and Jack get where you're going, and then fly around and melt some ice while looking large and terrifying."

"While an entire army is targeting you with their spears and arrows." The sarcasm was heavy.

He shrugged. "I'll burn hot enough that ninety-nine percent of it will melt or burn before it gets close enough to graze me."

"And the one percent that won't?"

"Will be so mangled beyond recognition that it won't be any sort of threat to my scales. Come here."

He pulled me fully against his chest, and for a minute I let myself sink against him. But since Alger-Aodh had given him back his control, he felt less like the Cole I'd come to care about so deeply.

"Let me feel your heat," I whispered, desperate to let his warmth encompass me and give me a fleeting sensation of safety.

His skin blazed through his clothes—still tattered and strung precariously together with the magic from our trip to the river.

"Mmm. I love feeling your fire." I curled my arms around him, laying my cheek against his chest where his heart beat steadily, pumping warmth with every movement.

"You gave me an entirely new sort of fire." His lips brushed the point of my ear. I shivered. "You cold?" He sounded surprised.

"No. It wasn't that sort of shiver."

"Oh." He smiled and tipped my face up before his face became serious again. "Please, please, please be careful out there."

"You, too."

Heedless of the other students and teachers milling around us, or the scandal our public display would likely cause, Cole kissed me hard and fast. Still, his lips were against mine long enough that I tasted his fear, his fire, and his warning. Matching it with my own tangle of emotion, I hugged him tight as he pulled his lips away.

"I do hope this isn't the sort of education the Academy is known for in the future," Jack interrupted.

Reluctantly we broke away, both grinning despite the circumstances. Jack smiled fondly at the pair of us.

"It's time." Jack stepped closer and shook Cole's hand. "Fly high and flame wide. Carry the fire-drake mantle well." Sadness touched his eyes.

"I will." Cole nodded. "I want to hear the crack of earth from the battlements."

Jack's whiskers showed his lips as they pulled up, banishing his sorrow. "I'll help you up on your beast, Aspen."

"Thanks, Jack. Cole, I'll see you soon."

"Without question." His fingers squeezed mine once more.

And then there was a wall of supple golden fur and feathers staring me in the face.

CHAPTER 40

COLE

My gut clenched and my heart constricted as Aspen walked away from me and towards a mammoth-sized flying cat sporting a few feathers and a beak.

So help me, I'd roast it to cinders if he so much as scratched her. Part of me was worried that she'd fall off mid-flight. My heart relaxed a fraction as the great animal bowed low to her and sunk down to the stones on his belly so she could climb astride.

She'd changed out of Anna Beth's long skirt and wore the one she'd come here in—and her legs were gloriously exposed, although I was pretty sure I was not the only one admiring a stunning view of skin. I bit back a grin, randomly wondering if we'd change the styles and fashions before we left.

Aspen settled on the golden back, her legs gripping the creature's neck in front of its wings. Her hands had a white-knuckle grip on the tufts of thick tawny hair growing out of the gryphon's ears.

Our eyes met one more time and we nodded solemnly to each other. This was it.

It was my turn.

Unsure if my clothes could withstand any more of the full force of my heat, I crept into the shadows of the tower on the battlements and stripped.

Almost wishing the cold air would chill me enough for a shiver, I shoved the errant thought aside and stepped out only far enough to spread my arms and let my shift take over.

Flames ran hot and potent down my arms and to my fingers. Tipping my head back, I let the fire ride up and over my body. Pulsing, aching, the hot-knife sensation of scales broke out over my form as they shoved forward and replaced my skin. As my limbs stretched to impossible new heights, I stepped up on the battlement edge and leaped, completing my shift and spreading wings that rivaled the sun.

Cries of terror and awe broke out from the Academy below me as I swooped into the air, positioning myself between the army and the school.

The shouts of the enemy on the mountain carried to me on the wind, and I flapped my wings three times, soaring straight up into the air.

Slitting my eyes and focusing on the army, I let out a wicked battle cry that cowered half the troops on the mountain even before I careened towards them. I blew a stream of fire around the base of the mountain closest to the school, wanting to draw attention to myself, and away from the two gryphons that blended into the shadows of the still rising dawn. My flames acted like a barrier between the river and the school. Between Lord Broderick's men and the Academy—and all the ideals it represented.

I had to give Aspen and Jack time.

I wheeled around, letting loose another round of fire into the air and shrieking loud enough to rattle the ground.

Circling nearer the mountain, I got a clearer view of the men assembled. There were a lot of them. More than I'd anticipated, even though I knew there had to be a full company based on what we'd overheard in the tunnels.

"Archers!" A commander ordered the troops below, the word just barely audible over the *swoosh* of my wings.

I was close enough to see the men ready a volley. Flapping higher, I put myself farther out of range. Not that arrows were any great threat to me.

"Fire!"

Crap!

Unless they were tinged in magic. Which these were.

I had assumed Lord Broderick's men would have no more magic than the Academy did. I flew a tight circle and let loose another stream of fire, anger roiling through me, heating me even hotter.

The flames melted most of the magic-tipped arrows, but a few still zipped past me, and one came within an inch or two of my left wing.

Beating against the smoke, I took myself even higher, the clouds sizzled into nothingness around me. I should be out of arrow reach now, although with that much magic at their disposal, things could get ugly. Since Magik Prep didn't have stores of magic, it honestly hadn't occurred to me that Lord Broderick's men might have access to it. I squinted through the haze of flames, eyeing the enemy soldiers.

I didn't want to kill anyone. I had enough guilt on my conscience. But if it came down to it, I wasn't sure I'd have a choice. The little dot left by Alger-Aodh's thumb pulsed on my forehead.

He must have known this was coming. There was a reason he'd chosen me, passed on his blessing. There had to be a reason he left me to defend the Academy instead of doing the job himself. I let the thought fill me with confidence as I leveled out for another pass. I let my anger rise, anger at Alger-Aodh's loss, anger at these men, anger that they were shooting at me, anger that they would try to take Aspen if they found her.

Now I was good and properly mad.

Letting out a shriek that made the trees shudder, I dove. Opening my fire lung, I purged.

A thick column of red and orange flame tore up the ground as I flew over the side of the mountain. Trees caught fire and men screamed.

And then I screamed, too. A giant magic-wrapped boulder crashed into me. I felt more than heard a great crack. Agony thrashed through me, though I wasn't sure if it was a rib or scales that had been damaged—but I was certain there was damage.

Pulling my wings up, a cry escaped as I hauled my injured carcass back into the skies.

This was not good.

I tried to open my fire lung. It didn't budge. Panic clawed at me as pain seared through my left side. Whatever that projectile had been wrapped in had doubled the impact of the boulder. I suspected they had a trebuchet hidden in the trees at the side of the mountain. Because I hadn't burned through the magic on the covering, the projectile had slammed into me with all its force and then some. And it had somehow welded my fire lung shut.

My body screamed in pain as my wings beat heavily against the air. Cradling my injured side with one scaly claw, I flew out of range.

Gasping and sputtering, I dragged in air, desperately trying to reinflate my fire lung. Without my fire lung, how was I going to melt all the ice in time?

Terror joined the panic and the pain, and a bellow of frustrated anguish escaped my lips.

Crack!

The earth shuddered and the slicing of ancient rock echoed beneath me.

The ice.

CHAPTER 41

Cole made a beautifully terrifying streak of fire across the inky sky as he surged off the battlements and into the greying light towards the enemy.

My stomach dipped as the gryphon tilted to better catch the draft Cole's wings caused. The wind stole the gasp from my lips as the creature steadied us then sped like a magicked missile over the ground. Flying close to the ground and in the shadows lessened my fear of flying on the gryphon. There was a shorter distance between me and the ground in the likely event I fell off.

Remembering to hang on to my ride instead of clapping a hand over my sensitive ears, I flinched as Cole screamed into the dawn. The shouts of the enemy carried over and a shiver worked down my spine.

I glanced at Jack, flying parallel to me. His back was bent, hunched over his gryphon, hands relaxed and face intent. He glanced over and nodded at me. His creature veered off, taking him to the far side of the mountain.

An emotional chill swept over my heart. I wished again for the hundredth time that Anna Beth had been convinced of our cause. We needed her. I worried that Jack and I would not be enough to carve the entirety of the Chasm before we were discovered. If we were found...I shuddered and shut off that line of thinking.

We had to survive. We had to succeed.

If we didn't, I would have no future to go home to. Neither would Cole.

"Archers!"

My heart constricted as I turned horrified eyes to the mountain. There was enough light from the rising sliver of sun and Cole's flames to clearly see hundreds of men aim giant long bows in the air towards Cole.

"No!"

The tips of the arrows were wrapped in different colors.

Magic.

Cole screeched and wheeled a tight circle and shot straight up into the air where he turned and let loose a stream and heavy flames. A few of the arrows still made their way to Cole, though I didn't think any had struck him.

"Faster," I whispered to the gryphon. My arms were jerked as the creature bent its head and went so fast little icicles formed at my temples where the water from my eyes leaked out.

One more bend and we were there. The gryphon landed lightly on his heavily taloned paws. I slid awkwardly to the ground, my legs all bendy like rubber bands.

Twitching as a thick shadow flew over me, I hit the ground in a crouch, palms outstretched, ready to freeze someone or something into oblivion.

Instead, my mouth dropped open as a second gryphon landed and Anna Beth slid gracefully off its back.

"You cannot stop me, Anna Beth," I whispered, fear that she'd try to stop me and that I'd have to hurt her ran up my spine.

Her shoulders dropped in a heavy sigh. "I'm not here to stop you. I'm here to help you. Father is right. This is his dream, not mine, but it's a dream that is important. Magik Prep is important. Without it, there's no other place for all the different races to be together, or to learn from each other. And I think this," she waved her arm towards the army, "proves that we need each other and should not fear one another."

A little noise of relief escaped my throat.

"Where do you need me?" she asked.

That snapped me back. "Your dad is on the far side. I'm supposed to start here. Can you go halfway between here and the river? Send ice down as hard and big as you can. We need to crack this wide enough that they can't easily swim across. Use the river water, too, if you need."

"All right. Aspen, for what it's worth, I'm sorry."

"Thanks. Get going!"

With a grin, she lithely hopped back astride her gryphon, and they were off.

Putting my palms flat on the ground, I searched again for Cole.

Fire plumed in front of him as he tore up the mountainside. His wings were an inferno behind him, his tail a whip of lightning.

With one last look at him, I closed my eyes and let the ice inside me free. Great sheets of it crashed into the earth. More and more, I let the freeze course through me, raw, frigid, and powerful. Down into the depths of the earth.

I sensed water far below the earth's surface. Reaching for it with all my power, I drew it up, froze it, expanded it, and moved the earth aside.

A shudder rippled under my feet, and I knew Jack or Anna Beth had started pushing their ice into the earth as well.

A harsh bellow broke my concentration. My eyes flew to Cole. His wings sagged as he gripped his side, yellow and blue flutters of magic trailing from the spot. They soon shriveled against the heat of Cole's body.

He was hurt.

Somehow, they'd done something, and he was wounded.

Panic lodged a jagged rock in my throat and tears threatened. He was still flying, flapping crookedly, taking himself higher and higher, out of range.

Tearing air into my chest, I used my distress to push my fear into ice, shoving it deeper into the ground.

At last, I was met with the sound of beginning success as a fissure burst beside me, glistening with ice. Leaping nimbly to the side, I kept my eyes riveted on Cole as he thrashed in the cloud layers, steam billowing around him.

Tasting blood, I realized I'd bitten my lip, tucked between my teeth. Carelessly wiping my mouth on my sleeve, I continued pouring more and more of myself into the ground, widening the crack and the layer of ice.

The earth rumbled and trembled.

A loud *rip* cut through the weak sunlight.

The screech of an eagle wrapped in the roar of a lion echoed in my chest and rang in my ears. Flinching, my hands came away from the earth.

My gryphon rolled to its back, tongue lolling out of its mouth, arrow embedded in its chest.

I whirled around in time to see a man step out of the shadows, arrow nocked and aimed at my heart.

In slow motion, I watched his fingers loose the shaft, the arrow curved as it slipped its string, on trajectory straight for my chest.

Cole shrieked somewhere in the distance. My mind jerked back to the present and to the arrow rushing me to my impending death.

With a flick of my right wrist, I brought a frigid wind rushing to the arrow, knocking it off course, and landing with a heavy *thunk* into a tree trunk a few paces away.

The man growled and drew another arrow back.

In desperation, I let a shard of ice fly. It embedded in the man's forehead. Blood streamed from the wound as the man sank to his knees, brown eyes watching the sky as the life ebbed from him. He fell face down on the frozen ground.

I heaved up the entire contents of my stomach.

The ground shook beneath me. Shakily, I rose to my feet, stretching my arms out to keep my balance.

There was enough light now to see the span of ice in the ground. I could see Anna Beth's gorge of ice racing towards me, splitting the earth in two like a ship cutting through waves. Glancing opposite, the river was a solid snake of ice and reaching towards me. I needed more. The ice beneath me must be wider. With renewed purpose, I set my hands on the ice and let my horror, inner turmoil, and choking guilt flood into the earth.

More and more and more, the ice flowed and the fissure in the earth widened until I stood on a glassy lake of frozen water. The mountain trembled and trees creaked and crashed down. The earth groaned and shuddered.

Men on the mountain were realizing what we'd done—that they were surrounded by ice. Orders were shouted, bodies scrambled, and I realized with no small amount of alarm, that I was stranded out here on the ice with no gryphon to take me back to the safety of the Academy.

Cole was still a ball of flames inside the steaming atmosphere, though most of the clouds had cleared around him. I had to move. All the ice had to be melted before the men could make it down the sides of the slope and get across to the school.

Slipping on the ice in my haste, I stumbled and clawed my way to my feet. It was now a race against time. I had to make it back to the Academy or I'd risk getting myself lost in the Chasm as Cole finished it.

Cole dipped against the morning sky. He still clutched his side, his wings flapped irregularly, one drooping lower than the other.

Adrenaline kicked my heart up another notch and I ran for all I was worth.

Lightning streaked from Cole's eyes as a wild scream tore from his throat. Something was wrong.

"Cole!" I panted between puffs of air as I ran and stumbled across the slick ice.

"Aspen!" Looking up, I stumbled and fell hard, scraping my knee as relief was a sweet rush through my middle. "Grab my hand!" Anna Beth yelled from atop her gryphon.

I leaped up, stretching my hands out as far as I could reach. Anna Beth's gryphon plunged lower, and Anna Beth caught my wrist. The speed of the gryphon helped her hoist me up behind her.

I clung for dear life. She scooted up farther on the animal's neck.

"Put your legs over his wings," she shouted against the wind whistling by us.

I scrambled, my skirt flying up, my fingers numb, but managed to get my legs wrapped in front of the golden wings. Clasping my hands around Anna Beth, we took off, the gryphon shooting into the sky and racing back towards the Academy.

With my heart thundering in my chest and my head aching, my eyes found Cole.

White hot streaks of phoenix fire blazed from his eyes. Why wasn't he shooting great plumes of fire from his mouth? Smoke curled around him—from the wound in his chest.

All around and below us, the crack of the ice, the crash of earth, the cries of the army, rose to meet us. It was deafening.

"Almost there," Anna Beth called over her shoulder.

The beige stones of the Academy walls soon materialized in front of us, cheers sounding from the battlements as whirls of magic and different creatures crowded the walls. Fists pounded the air while magic sizzled in the ether. Whoops and hollers of triumph reached a crescendo as we flew over the wall and drifted gracefully to the ground.

I bounded off the gryphon's back, legs like stretched out springs, and staggered my way to the stairs that would lead me to the ramparts.

I had to see Cole.

Anna Beth was hot on my heels. We stood side by side, hands clutching at the crenelations and rough stones as we searched for Cole and Jack.

Cole was a dark blaze of flames and smoke. His scales glowed with pent up heat as his injured side belched black smoke into the air. His eyes bore down white fury on the ice that immediately surrendered to boiling, steaming froth the instant his phoenix fire touched it. Great geysers of steam billowed as the searing hiss and pop of the melting ice echoed across the plains despite the noise of the panicked army and the cheers from those within the Academy.

I could make out the army scrambling around on the hilltop. Some shot ineffective arrows towards Cole, others tried to put out fires. Many slumped in defeat.

A great ocean of water churned and boiled around the island—the Chasm had been formed. The island was cut off.

With one more blast of white rage from his eyes, Cole turned and painstakingly made his way back towards the Academy. Heart in my throat, I clambered back down the stairs and reached the bottom just as Jack and his gryphon landed.

"The drake is injured. Get a stretcher and make a way to the infirmary!" Jack called as he slid to the ground near me.

A great shadow blocked out the sun and a sound like thunder rumbled from deep in his chest as Cole drifted over the walls, his tail knocking into the rock with a loud crack that made me flinch and had creatures ducking for cover from the live flames and tumbling rock.

His eyes found mine and the fight seemed to leave him. His eyes slid shut and his form shimmered. Before he was fully on the ground, he was completely in his human skin. His body bounced sickeningly against the grass, and he lay still, face down, naked, a nasty purple-black bruise wrapped around his left side like a mass of poisonous clinging vine.

I reached him first.

"Cole?" I whispered. Tiny ice crystals fell on his skin, and I blinked back my tears. Gently, I reached out and touched his hair. The green grass beneath him withered and hissed.

He was hot. Too hot. Too hot even for Cole.

"Cole, can you hear me?" Somehow the hysteria stayed out of my voice. Quickly I iced the ground beneath him to keep the dried grass from catching.

A strangled grunt sounded somewhere in his chest. Jack was beside us with Cole's shirt I'd mended.

"Turn him. Carefully," Jack instructed.

Mindful of his injured side and labored, wheezing breathing, Jack and I eased him onto his back.

Cole groaned, his face contorted in silent agony. Jack threw the shirt over Cole's waist.

"Lung," Cole rasped, eyes still shut. "Freeze...me."

"Where?" My hands fluttered frantically but helplessly, desperate to help him, but afraid to touch him.

"Fire lung...Shut...I'll explode." He wheezed as smoke trickled from his mouth and a cloud of it rose angrily from his bruised flesh.

"His fire lung is shut!" Jack shouted. "Stand back! Everyone! Someone get the salamander!"

I was glad Jack seemed to know what Cole meant, because I was completely at a loss. Ice chips fell from my face in earnest now, sizzling up in a waft of steam when they landed on Cole.

"Jack, what's wrong? How do we fix him?" My voice hitched, grief and terror leaking out.

"His fire lung is shut. He can't get it open. If we can't force it open, his fire inside will explode and kill him, and probably us, too," Jack said with an edge of panic to his voice.

"But he can go for weeks without purging, why is this so much worse?" This couldn't be happening. Cole was going to be just fine. He *had* to be.

"Because heat can escape into the rest of his body when his fire lung is open. But when it's shut, it builds until it can't hold anymore. He's already held it in longer than he should have—he finished melting the ice first." Snowflakes clouded above Jack as he bowed his head in reverence. The other creatures had backed up, leaving Jack, Cole, and me in our own haze of anguish.

I gripped Cole's hand, but he barely stirred.

Duri came bounding over the grass, tripping near us, and sprawling on the ground, but holding a metal cage aloft.

"It's here! The salamander!" he puffed.

"Go! Stand back," Jack ordered sternly.

Anna Beth whimpered beside us. I hadn't even realized she'd come down from the wall behind me.

"What's that?" I asked as Jack carefully drew the cage even with his eyes.

"This is one of the rarest creatures of legend. A fire salamander. They live in the heart of volcanos. They can sense fire and feed on its energy. Of all of us here at the Academy, this little fellow is the one most capable of finding and freeing Cole's flames inside his fire lung."

"Why do you have one here?" In horrified fascination, I watched as Jack opened the cage door and tipped the little orange, red, and yellow lizard-looking creature onto Cole's chest. It was the same creature Alger-Aodh had had in his breast pocket that last night in the library.

Cole wheezed and I gripped his hand harder, ice falling from my eyes.

"Because he was Alger-Aodh's pet," Jack said solemnly.

I hardly dared breath as the little creature sniffed, flicked the air with a little forked tongue of flame, and started nosing around near the angry bruised flesh.

"We should back up," Jack said softly.

"I won't leave him." I sniffed, stubbornly refusing to leave Cole's side.

"Very well." Jack leaned back but settled next to me on his haunches in the burnt grass.

The little salamander sniffed again and took a twitching step forward. Cole moaned, a strangled noise deep in his throat, as the tiny creature prodded the top of his purpled side.

I bit back a cry.

The salamander turned around, looked over his shoulder, and gave a smart *thwap* of his tail down on the middle of Cole's abused flesh.

With a gurgled shriek like a kraken on the hunt, Cole's head spasmed hard against the ground and the little creature skittered to Cole's mouth as Cole rolled like he might retch.

"He's choking!" I cried in terror.

"No, he's not, but get ready to use your ice again if you won't back up!" Jack put an arm in front of me as if to protect me.

Even as Jack finished, Cole coughed a great wracking wet noise, and then a roar that shook the foundations of the school echoed in the stillness of the meadow.

Cole flipped flat on his back, his eyes wide in shock. His mouth opened, and his whole chest lurched forward as a geyser of flames threw itself into the heavens with a deafening boom.

The little salamander crawled onto Cole's bottom lip, basking in the flames that should have incinerated it. I threw my free hand up, putting a wall of freeze between Cole's flames and me. I'd never imagined a heat so intense.

For several agonizing minutes, Cole purged and purged until not even ashes or cinders remained.

"Cole?" I ventured breathlessly once he lay still, utterly spent.

CHAPTER 42

COLE

For the first time I could ever remember, I felt my flames. The havoc, the pain, the searing rawness they left behind. My throat burned, my head throbbed, my body ached. But I was blessedly empty. My fire lung was open, and I was purged. Totally. And I hurt. All over.

My eyes focused on Aspen's face hovering over mine.

Nothing had ever looked so beautiful.

"Did we do it?" My voice croaked, and a wisp of smoke came out with my words.

"Yeah. We did." Her chin quivered and a few little ice crystals fell from her eyes. I tried to move my arm to swipe them away but groaned instead when the movement sent a wave of agony up my side and black dots spangling the corners of my vision.

"Don't try to move. You're pretty banged up," she said. "You've got a pretty impressive war wound." She gave me a watery smile.

I groaned again. "Yeah. I can tell."

A tiny amphibious face popped right up into mine and startled me hard enough it jarred my side again.

"Ah! What are you?"

It flicked a little forked tongue of flames at me.

"There's a fire salamander here?" Through the haze of pain and grogginess, I smiled at the tiny creature as it cocked its head at me.

"He belonged to Alger-Aodh. He saved your life," Jack said softly as he sat next to Aspen.

"Just how much of the future did he see?" I asked.

"More than I think any of us realized." Jack's smile was sad, but content.

"If it had been Alger-Aodh up there with a welded fire lung, he would have had no phoenix fire to melt the ice. It had to be you, Cole. Any other fire-drake would have been useless," Anna Beth whispered, awe on her face.

A sense of portent filled my chest, leaving behind a bittersweet pang of conviction, wonder, and regret.

CHAPTER 43

ASPEN

With some clever magic manipulation, Cole was on the mend by the end of the day. He was still stiff and sore, but he was whole and grateful. We both were. The Academy, its ideals, and its freedom were saved. So was the future.

King Trindon arrived two days later with an array of gryphon and Pegasus riders that was so impressive that no story could ever fully capture its magnificence. Cole and I watched King Trindon's men from one of the upper towers where we'd first discovered the green strand of magic. It felt like that was years ago.

The king's men rounded up the beaten soldiers with no trouble. After being stranded for two days and utterly cut off from reinforcements, none seemed to have the energy to oppose King Trindon.

I stared out at the island, water still lapping against its edges and spreading out over vast portions of the plains between this early version of the Chasm and the Academy. A grin tipped one side of my mouth, looking at my unexpected contribution to history.

"I think it's time to go home," Cole murmured softly into my hair.

I sighed. "I'll miss some things about this time."

"Me, too."

Hugh, Alger-Aodh's little fire salamander, poked his head out of Cole's pocket. The little creature had stayed with Cole every minute since he'd landed on Cole's chest.

"I think Hugh wants to come with you." I smiled affectionately at the little beast.

"You think that's wise?"

"He'll starve if we leave him here. There's no one else who gets hot enough to feed him properly."

"I would hate to leave him behind. And he would come in handy when I need to purge."

Smiling, I leaned my head against Cole's shoulder. "You know, I think you were right," I murmured.

"Yeah? About what?" His hand stroked down my arm.

"I think it would be smart to leave a healthy supply of magenta magic floating around. So far as we know, we're the only ones that can create it. There's never been another fire-drake phoenix hybrid with your same color of magic. Let alone another one that paired up with a frost fairy. And if we don't make more magenta magic now, there won't be any back in our time when we need it. Maybe the battle's outcome would have been different if we hadn't found it." The magnitude of the whole thing still made me dizzy to think about.

"I'm always up for exposure," Cole said with a cocky twist of his lips as his hand slid down my back.

"Cole, are we still going to be together when we get back to our time?" I needed to know. Our time seemed so far away from this moment. Would going back alter everything that had grown between us?

He pulled back, his black brows drawing together. "Don't you want to be?"

"Yes." My heart ached at the thought of not being with Cole.

"Good. You had me worried there for a second." He brushed a strand of hair behind my ear. "I don't ever want to be with anyone else. Only you." His eyes were black obsidian, the irises crackling with heat—the kind that I wanted to singe me.

I reached up on tip toe and put my lips on his.

We kissed in the tower. We kissed a lot more in the library. We kissed again in the tunnels. Anyplace we thought might be appropriate to store our specifically colored magic. And because kissing Cole was wonderful.

He added color, light, and heat to my life. My life before Cole had been a beautiful frozen sea of crystalline lights and ice. But Cole brought a spark that set the frozen parts of me alive. I never wanted to lose that spark.

When the time came for us to say goodbye, I was surprised how bittersweet it was. I longed for home but being in this time had changed me irrevocably. It had left a mark on my heart as surely as I had left my mark on this version of the Academy. Magic defense classes were instated by order of King Trindon himself after seeing what shared and hybrid magic accomplished. I'd even seen a few surreptitiously raised hemlines. Mistress Penwig might have her work cut out for her, investigating hem lengths for any shocking glimpses of ankles.

Tiny crystals fell from my eyes. Jack looked proudly at us as a father might have. I suppose he technically was my father—my forefather at least, since my line descended directly from his son. I wished I could have met him while we were here.

"I am so glad and so proud to have known you both." He gathered us both to his chest and hugged us tight. A few extra ice crystals joined mine as Cole cleared his throat uncomfortably.

"I'm sorry I...wasn't as supportive as I should have been," Anna Beth wrapped her arms around me.

"That's all right. You came through and saved the day in the end." I smiled at her.

"I was jealous of you, you know. Your confidence, your," she shrugged, "knowledge of the world. That Cole liked you." Her cheeks heated. "But taking my own insecurities and fear out on you was wrong, and I'm sorry."

"Anna Beth, you will have a long life, and from all accounts, you have your own adventures and your own love."

She beamed.

Maybe I shouldn't have told her. But I wanted to leave her with hope.

We took one last look around us, shared one last hug with Jack and Anna Beth, then walked to the place on the green where we'd first fallen through time.

"Ready?" Cole asked. His cheeks were flushed, and his eyes sparked.

"As ready as I'll ever be."

He nodded. Then he bent and brushed his lips across mine. "For luck," he whispered.

I kissed him back. "For luck," I repeated.

Carefully unfolding the biggest strand of the magenta magic we'd made I gripped my end and held the other out to Cole.

"I hope this works."

"Me, too." He licked his lips. "All right. We do it just like we did on the way here—just like Stormwalker described in his journal." Hugh poked his head out of Cole's pocket. Cole gently pushed him back down. "It's a long trip, Hugh. Best stay covered. Ready, Aspen?"

"Think about home and twist on three," I said, nerves ratcheting up my spine.

"One. Two. Three!"

I gave a hard twist and pictured the green as I'd last seen it, with Kasin and Arietta's faces hovering in the foreground, sneers bending their lips into unsympathetic lines.

There was a hard tug on my hair, and spangles of color burst in front of me as my body became weightless and careened into a free-fall.

"Oooph!" The wind left me in a rush as my backside connected hard with the ground. Blinking, I jerked to sitting, wincing as my muscles protested and my head spun.

"Cole?"

He groaned. "Are we here? Did we make it?"

Our strip of magenta magic fizzled into ash in the grass between us. I reached for his hand as my heart hammered.

"Ah, isn't that sweet. The Fire Freak and the Ice Queen have found each other. Maybe you guys can do each other some good!" Kasin hollered. Arietta tittered beside him, looking coy trying to hide her smirk behind her pudgy, daintily raised hand.

My blood boiled. But Cole yelled before I could even open my mouth to retort.

"Hey Kasin, you still limping, or you need a spurt of heat to thaw your balls?" A sphere of fire plumed to life in Cole's open palm.

Kasin's face drained of all color as Arietta's eyes grew large in her face. She glanced at me then turned to Kasin, smelling an even more sensational story than the one she had.

Kasin took one look at Arietta's face then turned and ran back across the green to the main building.

Arietta turned excitedly to me. "Oh, my stars. What happened?"

My eyes narrowed and snow formed on my fingertips.

To her credit, Arietta had high self-preservation instincts and beat it across the lawn to follow after Kasin.

"We made it," I breathed the words once Arietta had disappeared back into the building.

"We did." Cole squeezed my fingers. "Can I take you on a real date now that we're back in our own time and since Alger-Aodh's blessing seems to be holding?"

"So long as it's not a party on the island."

"It's a deal."

His lips closed over mine and my eyes slid shut.

A throat cleared and we lurched apart.

My cheeks flooded with color as Professor Rashtin stood over us, one horse hoof pawing the ground.

"Historically speaking, kissing on school grounds in the middle of the day is frowned upon."

I couldn't help the giggle that bubbled up.

"Historically speaking, we could tell you a thing or two."

Hugh poked his head out of Cole's pocket and let out a little puff of smoke.

More from the world of Magik Prep Academy

Also From Magik Prep

Enjoy "Goggles," a Magik Prep Academy short story you can find in *Making Magik*.

Goggles

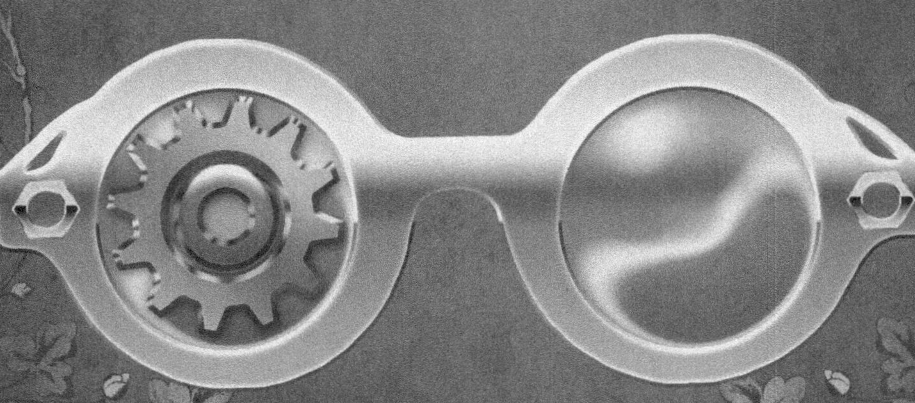

GOGGLES

I smelled like basilisk poop.

And Tatianna Everblaze was coming toward me with her gaggle of friends.

She was the most beautiful girl at Magik Prep Academy.

Her golden hair was tied back with a red ribbon that matched the occasional flames that rose in her eyes as her inner phoenix flashed. We were seniors this year, but I'd been a goner after the first time we'd had a freshman study session together. Happy fire flashed in her eyes as she laughed at something one of the girls said as they neared the basilisk barn.

I groaned. Half my face was still covered by stupid protective goggles. One peek from basilisk eyes and you'd be seeing a whole other type of flames. As in, a poof of smoke and you left nothing but ashes behind. While the goggles protected me from any accidental basilisk glaring, they did nothing for my facial features. The strap of the unwieldy glasses went around my head and made my pointed ears stick out nearly parallel to the floor. I looked more like a devil than an elf. But I was required to wear them at all times inside the barn. Safety first and all that.

I leaned my shovel against the pen where I'd been cleaning out the basilisk stalls. Scholarship students had to earn their keep. And if I wanted to graduate with the credentials to go on and study mythological biology at university, I had to pay my dues and scoop the poop.

But why did I have to do it in front of Tatianna?

"Owen?" Her voice sent shivers down my spine and mortification rushing to my face. I was the only one on duty at the stables this afternoon. I sighed. There was no hiding.

"Owen, are you back there?" she called again.

"Coming!"

I squared my shoulders and took a breath and ignored the acrid smell of the scat on my boots.

"Hi, Tatianna, Savannah, Sloane." I nodded politely, squirming inside as the goggles weighted down my face and made my nod some bobbling jiggle. "What can I do for you ladies?"

Savannah tittered. "Owen, your eyeballs are bigger than a cyclops' in those goggles."

Because I wasn't self-conscious enough already.

Tatianna elbowed her friend and glared. A lash of flames flicked in her irises.

"Ignore her, Owen," Tatianna said. I nodded again, unsure. "I heard the baby basilisks were starting to hatch. I was hoping to take a look at them." She smiled, her face hopeful.

She was speaking to me. My tongue froze.

"I'm writing a paper on the life cycle of the basilisk, when they develop their venomous glare and stuff. Is it okay if we go back to the nesting area? I promise we'll stay far away. I just want to observe a while." She smiled winningly.

"I," I cleared my throat. "That should be fine."

Awesomely brilliant thing to say.

"Come on, I'll take you back." I reached under the counter by the entrance and pulled out several pairs of goggles.

"Ugh. Really?" Savannah grumbled. "The babies aren't even dangerous."

"Rules are rules," Sloane chimed in. "You could get an expulsion if a professor caught you in here without them on. Besides, who knows when the mother might make an appearance?" Sloane was ever a rule follower.

The girls followed me down the hay strewn aisle to the back corner where the nest of eggs was kept. There'd been a few hatchlings today and they weren't much bigger than large earth worms.

"Wow. Why did you choose to do your report on these ugly little wiggly things?" Savannah asked as Tatianna crouched to get a better look.

"They're interesting! How many other creatures can destroy you with one look?" Tatianna said.

"Uh, anything spawned by Medusa?" Savannah retorted.

Tatianna rolled her eyes, her flames waving behind the lenses. "Owen, do you know how many hatched this morning?"

I swallowed as her red-brown eyes tracked to mine behind the hideous goggles. Even with the eyewear, she was stunning. The goggles magnified her eyes, their natural glimmer enhanced. It made my knees weak.

"I think three this morning. A few more this afternoon," I stammered.

She nodded and we fell silent as we watched the baby basilisks.

Savannah grabbed the shovel I'd been using earlier and used the wooden end to prod a clump of hay out by itself in the nest area.   "Is that a pile of...?"

"Stop!" I shouted.

Suddenly a loud hiss broke through the quiet of the barn and the hairs on the back of my neck stood on end.

"What is..." Savannah broke off with a scream as the mother basilisk launched herself straight for Savannah's face.

She flailed, her arm catching me just under the goggles.

"No!" I gasped as the momentum of her arm took the edge of the goggles off. I could smell the venom emanating from the creature. Scales appeared in front of my naked eyes as the creature catapulted towards me.

Sloane screamed.

"Oh, no you don't!" Tatianna's voice sounded far off.

She whipped off her goggles and a stream of white-hot flame jumped from her eyes and startled the mother basilisk.

It was the hottest thing I'd ever seen in my life. Literally and figuratively.

The basilisk slithered off, hissing and spitting.

Without words we legged it back to the barn entrance, quickly leaving the goggles on the desk and moving into the open air of the meadow beside the barn.

"Are you all right, Owen?" Tatianna asked, her flickering eyes full of concern that sent heat straight to my toes and had nothing to do with the inferno hiding inside her.

"I am, thanks to you," I admitted. I attempted a smile that she returned.

"Everyone else okay?" I asked. Sloane and Savannah nodded shakily.

"You girls go on back. I'll catch up," Tatianna nodded to her friends. Savannah still looked significantly shaken while Sloane looked smug as she glanced at us.

She took Savannah's arm and led her back toward the dormitories.

"That was an impressive display of flames back there," I said, swallowing hard. "Thank you. You probably saved my life." The gravity of the situation was not lost on me.

Tatianna shrugged and tucked the corner of her bottom lip between her teeth.

"I feel kind of guilty. You wouldn't have been in that position at all if I hadn't asked to see the baby basilisks."

"It's fine. They're not off limits. Besides, didn't you want to research them?"

"Well, yes." She hesitated and glanced sideways at me. "But that's not the real reason I wanted to come see them."

"It's not?" My eyebrows hitched up my forehead. She looked up at me shyly under her long lashes.

"I actually just wanted to come hang out with you. The basilisks were an excuse."

My mouth fell open like a drop-jaw ready to consume its prey.

"Say something, Owen."

"You don't need the basilisks as an excuse."

"Yeah?" Her whole face brightened, and my heart thundered.

"Yeah," I whispered back with a smile so wide my cheeks hurt.

Tentatively I reached out and brushed her fingers. Hers tightened around mine and her eyes lit with an entirely different kind of fire as her mouth tipped up.

"Although maybe I could wash off the basilisk poop before we hang out?"

She giggled and set my heart on fire.

THANKS

So many hours of dreams, of brainstorming, of creating, and possibly even a few tears have gone into the making of this book.

So many people jumped on board to help.

So many blessings.

Thank you to each one of you who volunteered to make this book what it is today.

It took me nearly ten years to write my first novel. I started writing it in the middle of a lot of pivotal life changes that just didn't leave a lot of time for writing. But because it took me so long to finish it, I assumed I was just one of those writers that took a really long time to write a book.

NaNoWriMo was around the corner, and I was intrigued by the idea of writing a whole novel in a month. I thought it sounded crazy. I also thought it sounded like an unbearable amount of stress to add to my already chaotic life.

I opted not to do NaNoWriMo, but a month or so before, I decided to challenge myself to write a novel over the course of two months. Which is nearly what NaNo does. But it felt like less pressure if I was the only one holding myself accountable.

I'd already spent a decent amount of time in the Magik Prep world writing short stories and thought maybe I could write a novel in that world. I set myself daily word counts that would allow me to finish a full-length novel within two months.

To my utter shock and delight, setting those manageable word counts allowed me to not only meet my goal, but exceed it. By the end of one month, I had the first draft of *Of Flame & Frost* completed. It was shorter than most standard YA novels, but I'd done it. I'd written a full book in one month.

Since then, it's seen many revisions, and there were several exceedingly helpful people that bettered it along the way. Mom, Lacey, Meghan, Jessica, Sarah, Brittany, Vanessa, and The Empress, THANK YOU. You guys were the team I needed to turn this into something fit for public consumption. Anne, thank you for all your advice and input on the technical end of things!

Morgan L. Busse, thank you so much for your kind words about my world and my story. They came at a time when I desperately needed them, and I'll be forever grateful. Alyssa and Vanessa, thank you, too, for your wonderful words. They are deeply appreciated.

Of Flame & Frost was a major turning point in my writing journey. I realized I *could* write more than one book every ten years. I also learned I shouldn't try writing one full-length story *every* month!

If you're still reading this, I'd like to challenge you to step out of your comfort zone. Set a reasonable goal for yourself, and then go reach for it. Even if you miss, you'll have learned something in the trying of it. Find your people, surround yourself with those who love you and want the best for you.

If you'd like to keep in touch, feel free to sign up for my infrequent newsletter over at www.ajskelly.com. If you feel like you just need some encouragement, you're welcome to email me at aj@ajskelly.com. I respond to every email.

Blessings,

-AJ

Pater, gratias ago tibi, quia donum verba.
Soli Deo Gloria

THE AUTHOR

 AJ Skelly, also writing as April J. Skelly, is an author, reader, and lover of all things fantasy, history, and fairy-tale-romance. And werewolves. She has a serious soft spot for them. As an avid life-long reader and a former high school English teacher, she's always been fascinated with the written word. She lives with her husband, children, and many imaginary friends who often find their way into her stories. They all drink copious amounts of tea together and stay up reading far later than they should. You can read more about her and her books at www.ajskelly.com or at ajskelly.substack.com. Find her on Instagram at @a.j.skelly or Readers of AJ Skelly on Facebook.

IF YOU WANT TO READ MORE BOOKS LIKE

OF

FLAME & FROST

QUILL & FLAME PUBLISHING HOUSE
HAS YOU COVERED

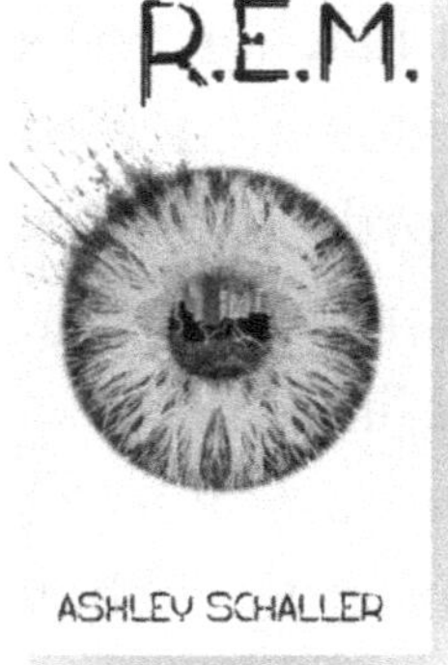

HEAT WITHOUT THE SCORCH

Quill & Flame
PUBLISHING HOUSE

www.quillandflame.com

Magik Prep Academy

www.ingramcontent.com/pod-product-compliance
Lightning Source LLC
Chambersburg PA
CBHW060850210726
48293CB00006B/1734